STAR TREK
STARSHIP SPOTTER

STAR TREK®
STARSHIP SPOTTER

ADAM "MOJO" LEBOWITZ

&

ROBERT BONCHUNE

WITH

JONATHAN LANE & ALEX ROSENZWEIG

POCKET BOOKS

New York   London   Toronto   Sydney   Singapore

An *Original* Publication of POCKET BOOKS

POCKET BOOKS, a division of Simon & Schuster, Inc.
1230 Avenue of the Americas, New York, NY 10020

ISBN: 0-7434-3725-X

First Pocket Books trade paperback printing November 2001

10   9   8   7   6   5   4   3   2   1

POCKET and colophon are registered trademarks of Simon & Schuster, Inc.

For information regarding special discounts for bulk purchases, please contact
Simon & Schuster Special Sales at 1-800-456-6798 or business@simonandschuster.com

Printed in the U.S.A.

INTRODUCTION

If I thanked everyone who helped make this book possible, this page would read exactly like Rob's, so just turn to the back of the book, read his acknowledgments, then turn back here.

I mean it.

Have you memorized the names? Good.

I sincerely appreciate the positive influence each one of you has had on our lives and this book. Without all of you, Rob and I wouldn't have made it this far and I hope you'll be there for us in the future (especially when we need to make bail next year for breach of contract if we don't make the deadline for *Unseen Frontier*). As for Doug Drexler—without you, corned beef, cheesecake and *Star Trek* just wouldn't be the same.

I know Rob would agree that what you're now holding represents our lives coming full circle; we both grew up on *Star Trek* and I can remember running to the bookstore with each trip to the mall and excitedly checking to see if they had any new *Star Trek* stuff! I lived vicariously through the *Technical Manual* for years, and I spent all my free time locked in my room, drawing the spaceships I saw on the book covers and dreaming I was aboard them.

Starship Spotter proves I never could quite get myself to *stop* drawing them. Back then I would have killed for a book that didn't just have a ship on the cover, but had one on every page.

Finally, that book exists.

Of course, I never would have imagined that I would be one of the people who produced it, but that's what *Star Trek* is all about—making the impossible happen.

These pages are filled with images of the real stars of *Star Trek*—the ships—and I applaud Pocket Books for realizing it was time to shine the spotlight on these oft-neglected celebrities. If you're a wide-eyed fan of any age, and this book is fuelling *your* dreams, just remember—if Rob and I could do it, so can you.

Mojo
June 2001

CONTENTS

STARFLEET SHIPS & FACILITIES

U.S.S. ENTERPRISE NCC-1701

CONSTITUTION-CLASS   FIRST COMMISSIONED: 2245

MISSION

Intended to be Starfleet's preeminent vessel for exploration, research, and defense, the *Constitution*-class starships were the largest and most ambitious design of their day. Engineering lessons learned in the designs of earlier starships were refined and incorporated into a new breed of starship capable of supporting a wide variety of missions. *Constitution*-class ships could effectively rise to the challenge of such diverse assignments as long-range exploration, scientific surveys, planetary defense, deep-space patrol, and expeditionary support. Captain Robert April once commented, ". . . a *Constitution*-class starship could do anything."

FEATURES

At the time it was commissioned in the mid-twenty-third century, the *Constitution*-class was the largest and most elaborate vessel of its type ever constructed. Fourteen science labs made it the most extensive mobile research platform ever sent into space by the Federation. The modularity of the *Constitution*-class design proved highly effective, so much so that only incremental changes in the overall vessel configuration were made over the following twenty-five years. It was not until the *U.S.S. Enterprise*'s upgrade in 2273 that large-scale redesigning of the *Constitution*-class occurred.

BACKGROUND

The second quarter of the twenty-third century marked a crucial shift in Starfleet's approach to vessel design, engineering, and construction. A major fleetwide modernization program proceeded to incorporate the use of standardized components such as primary hulls and warp-drive nacelles. The *Constitution*-class, commissioned in 2245, quickly emerged as the quintessential archetype of this program.

As originally proposed, the *Constitution*-class would have been a considerably smaller vessel. But as the Starfleet Corps of Engineers began to build on the lessons learned from starship studies commissioned in the 2230s, the design for the *Constitution*-class was enlarged. Ultimately, these enhancements led to such features as increased science and research capability and a larger hangar bay.

Bursting to the forefront of the wave of exploration in the latter half of the twenty-third century, these starships expanded the area of explored space by thousands of cubic parsecs. Of those original fourteen ships, only two had been lost by 2270, demonstrating the overall superiority of the design.

This class of starship is most commonly remembered for the initial five-year mission of Captain James T. Kirk and his crew. Under Kirk's command, the *Starship Enterprise* made first contact with the Organians, the Gorn, the Metrons, Excalbians, Melkotians, Kelvans, Thasians, and the First Federation. The crew survived multiple skirmishes with the Klingons, Romulans, and even Tholians. The *Enterprise* also tested Starfleet's first-ever multitronic computer system (M-5).

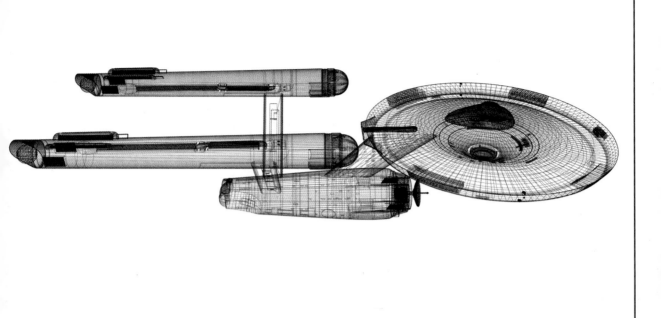

SPECIFICATIONS

Dimensions:
  Overall Length: 288.6 meters
  Overall Beam: 127.1 meters
  Overall Draft: 72.6 meters
Displacement: 190,000 metric tons
Crew Complement: 430 persons
Velocity*:
  Cruising: Warp Factor 6
  Maximum: Warp Factor 8
Acceleration*:
  Rest-Onset Critical Momentum: 17.14 sec
  Onset Critical Momentum-Warp Engage: 2.01 sec
  Warp 1-Warp 4: 1.02 sec
  Warp 4-Warp 6: 0.56 sec
  Warp 6-Warp 8: 2.21 sec

Duration:
  Standard Mission: 5 years
  Recommended Yard Overhaul: 18 years
Propulsion Systems:
  Warp: (2) PB-32 Mod 3 Circumferential Warp Drive Units
  Impulse: (4) SBE Subatomic Unified Energy Impulse Units
Weapons:
  2 447/54 Retractable Single Mount Phaser Emplacements
    (1 Bank/2 Each)
  2 Mk 12 Mod 2 Indirect-Fire Photon Torpedo Tubes
Primary Computer System: Daystrom Duotronic Processor
Primary Navigation System: Starmark Warp Celestial Guidance
Deflector Systems: R776/A3 Subsurface Hull Deflector
  Grid System
Embarked Craft: 5-7 Shuttlecraft (various classes)

*Velocity and acceleration figures reflect the rated specifications in the Original Cochrane Unit (OCU) warp scale as set prior to 2312, after which time Starfleet adopted the Modified Cochrane Unit (MCU) warp scale.

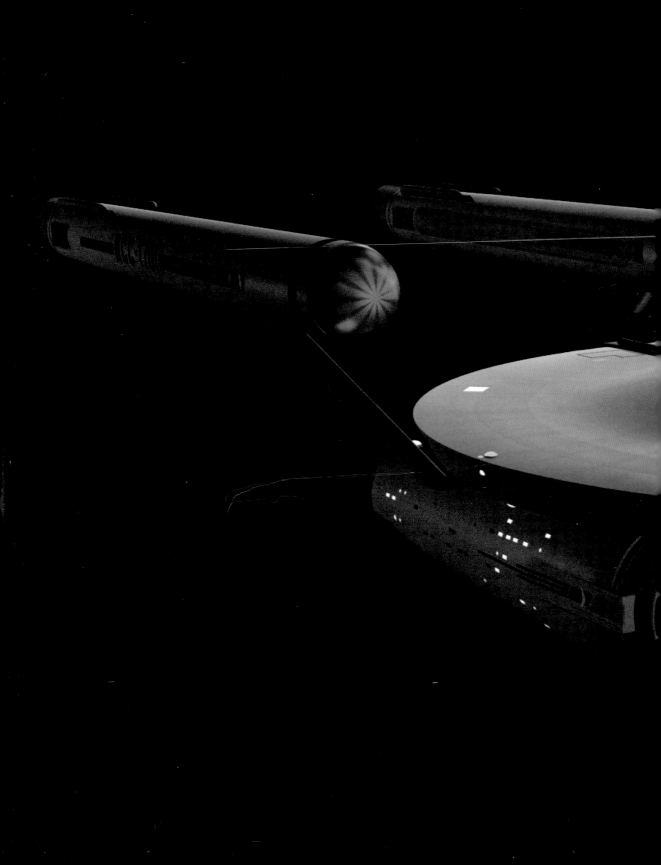

WORK BEE

GENERAL UTILITY CRAFT   FIRST COMMISSIONED: 2268

MISSION

Designed to support the construction and maintenance of starships and space stations, the Work Bee is an extremely versatile craft. conjunction with a myriad of specialized add-on modules, the Work Bee can perform a variety of missions, including but not limited to: car and passenger module carrying and transport, external construction and repair, observation and analysis. The value of this small craft can observed in the fact that from 2268 through to the present day—over 110 years—the Work Bee has remained in continuous service.

FEATURES

While essentially little more than an operator's cab, the critical feature of the Work Bee is the craft's modularity. The single-seat cockp can be attached to—or have attached to it—units such as a grabber sled, a welder unit, a "metal spinner" unit, cargo and passenger modu trains, and a host of other specialized modules. Adding to the Work Bee's versatility, the forward hatch can be easily opened, allowing a spac suited operator to leave the Bee to conduct an extravehicular activity (EVA) and then return to the craft for the trip back to base. The hatc can also be entirely disconnected and removed, should a task prove more efficient to perform with the craft unpressurized and open.

BACKGROUND

At first glance, the outer shell design of the Work Bee operating in 2377 is virtually identical to the shell of a Work Bee of a hundred yea earlier. Many of the internal systems have been upgraded and the range of modular attachments has expanded and progressed with advance ments in technology. But the general excellence of the Work Bee design has necessitated few improvements over the years, and Starflee planners confidently project that the Work Bee will continue in service well into the twenty-fifth century.

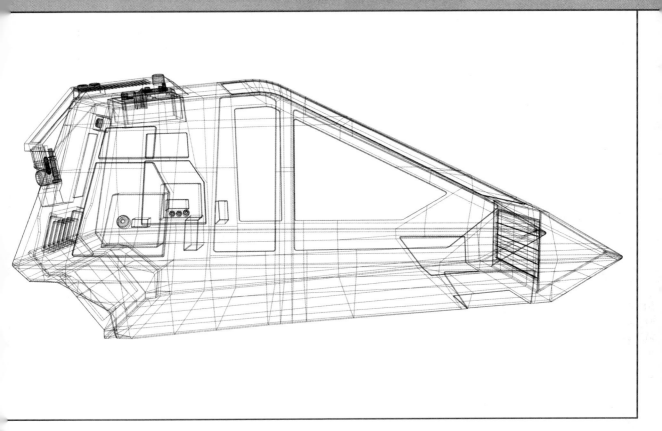

SPECIFICATIONS (2270)

Dimensions:
  Overall Length: 1.2 meters
  Overall Beam: 1.2 meters
  Overall Draft: 1.3 meters
Displacement: 2.23 metric tons
Crew Complement: 1 person
Velocity:
  Cruising: 7.9 km/sec
  Maximum: 8.2 km/sec
Acceleration:
  Rest-Maximum Velocity: 12.40 sec

Duration:
  Standard Mission: 6 hours
  Recommended Yard Overhaul: 11 months
Propulsion Systems:
  Maneuvering: (2)M-1020 Particle Beam Thrusters
  Reaction Control: (32) Pulsed Laser Thrusters
Weapons: NONE
Primary Computer System: 12K 1248 Integrated
  Support System
Primary Navigation System: 1248-I NavCom Add-On
Deflector Systems: NONE

U.S.S. ENTERPRISE NCC-1701

CONSTITUTION-CLASS (REFIT)   FIRST COMMISSIONED: 2273

MISSION

In 2270, the *U.S.S. Enterprise* returned to Earth amid much fanfare. At the same time, Starfleet had recently made a series of significa advancements in technology and was eager to incorporate these features into existing vessels. The stage was quickly set for the *Enterprise* get these cutting-edge improvements. This new design was created to be the premier exploratory vessel, while still serving as a front-line co bat vessel. Rushed into service in 2273 to intercept the threatening V'Ger probe, the *Enterprise* quickly proved the effectiveness of the n design. The vessel's subsequent successes across a diverse range of missions led to the implementation of this upgrade for the next forty yea

FEATURES

The refitted *Constitution*-class was a trailblazer. New equipment and features on this class of starship included the linear warp drive (whi became *the* standard design), advanced and upgraded transporters, a redesigned sickbay, an upgraded computer system, increased crew capa ity and comfort, and a new power system that fed directly from the primary matter/antimatter reactors to the phaser banks. In this syste the amount of phaser power was increased, but an initial design flaw cut power to the phaser banks if the warp drive was off-line. This ove sight nearly destroyed the *Enterprise* during the ship's initial mission and was subsequently corrected.

BACKGROUND

The refitted *Constitution*-class ushered in a renaissance in spacecraft technology. Indeed, elements of that improved design standa remain in use even a century later. The design became one of the most recognizable Starfleet vessels in history.

The *U.S.S. Enterprise* NCC-1701-A was likewise a refitted *Constitution*-class starship. To honor the *Enterprise* and her gallant crew, Starfle Command issued an administrative order specifying that from that point forward, each Federation starship to carry the name *Enterprise* wou also carry the ship's original registry number, with a consecutive letter-suffix indicating each new vessel. To date, five starships have carrie that number, the most recent being the *Sovereign*-class *U.S.S. Enterprise* NCC-1701-E.

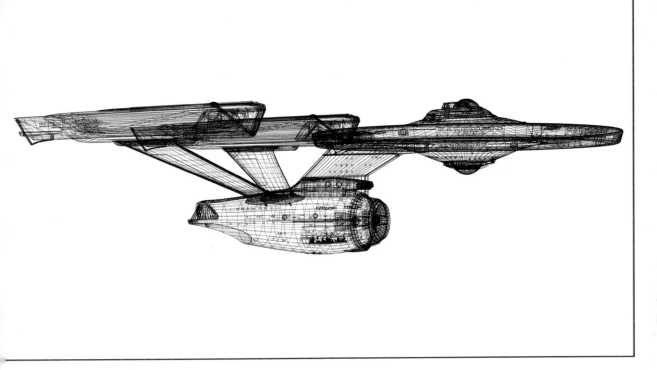

SPECIFICATIONS

Dimensions:
Overall Length: 304.8 meters
Overall Beam: 141.7 meters
Overall Draft: 71.3 meters
Displacement: 210,000 metric tons
Crew Complement: 500 persons
Velocity*:
Cruising: Warp Factor 8
Maximum: Warp Factor 12
Acceleration*:
Rest-Onset Critical Momentum: 8.51 sec
Onset Critical Momentum-Warp Engage: 1.12 sec
Warp 1-Warp 4: 0.78 sec
Warp 4-Warp 8: 0.67 sec
Warp 8-Warp 12: 2.13 sec
Duration:
Standard Mission: 5 years
Recommended Yard Overhaul: 22 years

Propulsion Systems:
Warp: (2)LN-64 Mod 3 Linear Warp Drive Units
Impulse: (2)RSM Subatomic Unified Energy Impulse Units
Weapons:
12 RIM-12C Independent Twin Mount Phaser Emplacements
(6 Banks/2 Each)
6 RSM-14B Single Mount Phaser Emplacements
2 Mk 6 Mod 1 Direct-Fire Photon Torpedo Tubes
Primary Computer System: Daystrom Duotronic III Processor
with Multitronic M-7 Supplement
Primary Navigation System: Warp Celestial Guidance
Deflector Systems: Primary Force Field and Deflector
Control System
Embarked Craft (Typical):
8 Work Bee General Utility Craft
4 Shuttlecraft (various classes)

Velocity and acceleration figures reflect the rated specifications in the Original Cochrane Unit (OCU) warp scale as set prior to 2312, after which time Starfleet adopted the Modified Cochrane Unit (MCU) warp scale.

U.S.S. MAJESTIC NCC-31060

MIRANDA-CLASS   FIRST COMMISSIONED: 2283

MISSION

One of Starfleet's most successful designs, the *Miranda*-class starship began its existence as a humble complement to the *Constitutio* class in the latter part of the twenty-third century. Compact and easily constructed, the *Miranda*-class made for a highly adaptable mul mission resource to augment the larger *Constitution*-class and *Excelsior*-class vessels. Its combination of versatility and ease of constructic allowed the *Miranda* to perform a variety of tasks, from combat to scientific research to support services and cargo transport. As a result this expansive utility, the class remained in service throughout the twenty-fourth century.

FEATURES

Miranda-class starships are a familiar design within Starfleet, notable for several distinctive features. The most visible and recognizab feature of the vessel is the bar mounted pulsephaser cannons. Developed as an outgrowth of mass-inversion research, these powerful weapor draw their power from plasma feeds directly off the main conduits running to the warp nacelles. The second most notable feature of th *Miranda*-class is its modularity. Interchangeable and removable elements allow the class to be utilized for a wide variety of missions, and t support equipment in varying configurations. As a result, *Miranda*-class starships have appeared in a number of arrangements, including ve sions with and without the bar module and configurations utilizing outboard mounted weapons and sensor units.

BACKGROUND

The success of the *Miranda*-class design began even before the *U.S.S. Miranda* was completed. The unique spaceframe concept was applie to a refit program for an existing fleet of frigates. Following closely after the highly effective *Constitution*-class refit program, the upgrad marked the first appearance of the configuration which would later become the *Miranda*-class. The new design proved so successful and ver satile, Starfleet moved rapidly to commission a number of vessels in this class. Although most of those early *Miranda*-class cruisers have lon since been decommissioned, as the class nears its centennial, Federation citizens will still see the familiar shape of a *Miranda*-class cruise from time to time, carrying on the proud tradition of a proven starship design.

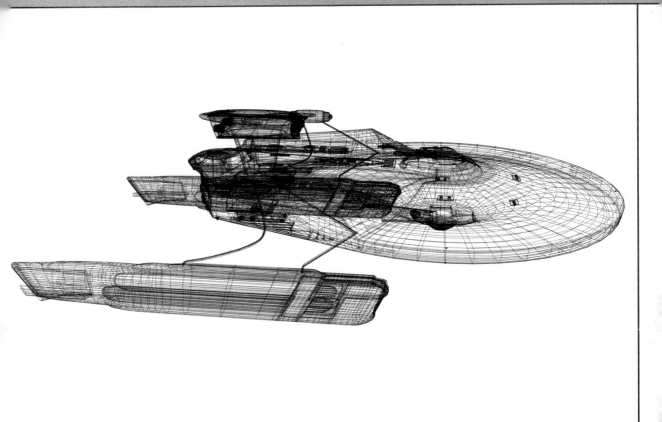

SPECIFICATIONS

Dimensions:
  Overall Length: 237.6 meters
  Overall Beam: 141.7 meters
  Overall Draft: 58.0 meters
Displacement: 150,000 metric tons
Crew complement: 360 persons (original configuration)
Velocity:
  Cruising: Warp Factor 7
  Maximum: Warp Factor 11
Acceleration:
  Rest-Onset Critical Momentum: 6.08 sec
  Onset critical Momentum-Warp Engage: 1.23 sec
  Warp 1-Warp 4: 0.81 sec
  Warp 4-Warp 7: 0.70 sec
  Wap 7-Warp 11: 2.42 sec
Duration:
  Standard Mission: 5 years
  Recommended Yard Overhaul: 19 years

Propulsion Systems:
  Warp: (2) LN-64 Mod 3 Linear Warp Drive Units
  Impulse: (2) RST Subatomic Unified Energy Impulse Units
Weapons:
  6 Type VII-12 Twin Mount Phaser Emplacements
    (6 Banks/2 Each)
  2 Multi-Directional Pulsephaser Pulse Cannons
  4 Mk 22 Mod 1 Direct-Fire Photon Torpedo Tubes
Primary Computer System: Daystrom Duotronic III Processor
  with Multitronic M-9 Supplement
Primary Navigation System: RAV/ISHAK Warp Celestial Guidance
Deflector systems: Primary Force Field and Deflector Control
  System
Embarked Craft (Typical):
  12 Work Bee General Utility Craft
  4 Shuttlecraft (various classes)
  1 Shuttlepod

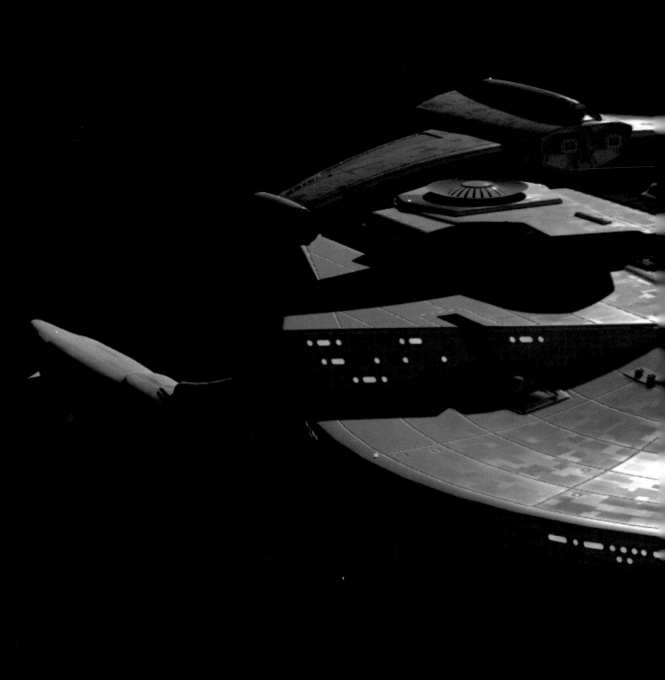

U.S.S *HONSHU* NCC-60205

NEBULA-CLASS   FIRST COMMISSIONED: 2357

MISSION

Considered by many to be the "little sister" to the *Galaxy*-class starship, the *Nebula*-class starship was designed to be more pragmat
Developed in parallel with the *Galaxy*-class, the *Nebula*-class shared many similar components and onboard technology features. The *Nebu*
class was designed to be easier to construct and maintain, and it could more readily serve in smaller in-systems, in patrol, tactical, and su
port roles. Adding to the ship's versatility was the modular mission-configurable pod, which could augment the ship's standard facilities f
a diverse array of mission profiles.

FEATURES

First and foremost, the *Nebula*-class distinguished itself as a compact, efficient design using established Starfleet components. But th
Nebula-class is best known for its large mission-configurable upper pod. With a number of variant configurations—including a tactical po
a large sensor pod, a cargo pod, and a probe pod—the *Nebula*-class could become a different starship for each mission. The *Nebula*-class
primary systems were carefully designed to be flexible, so as to function optimally for each type of mission the ship might undertake.

BACKGROUND

In the twenty-third century, the *Miranda*-class starship emerged as the more versatile alternative to the larger and more elaborate refit c
the *Constitution*-class starship. The *Nebula*-class developed the same relationship to the larger *Galaxy*-class. The *Nebula*-class quickly took i
place as one of the most common vessels in Starfleet. *Nebula*-class ships have participated in such actions as the blockade of Romulan suppl
lines to the Duras family during the Klingon Civil War, the Battle of Wolf 359, and many tactical engagements during the Dominion War.

In recent years, some of Starfleet's basic vessel technology elements have been evolving beyond the designs of the *Galaxy*- and *Nebula*
classes. Nevertheless, the practicality and effectiveness of the *Nebula*-class design is such that it is expected to remain a significant part o
Starfleet well into the twenty-fifth century.

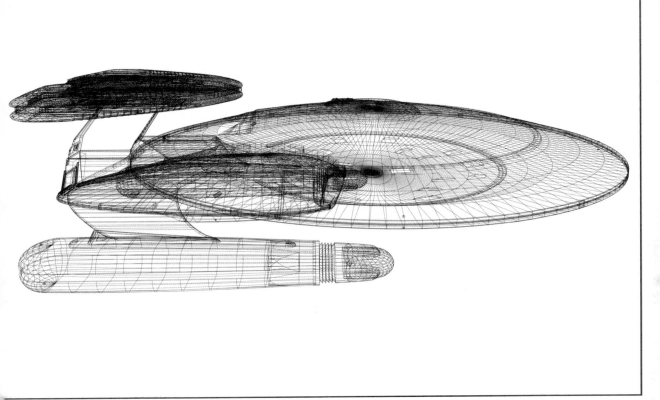

SPECIFICATIONS

Dimensions:
 Overall Length: 465 meters
 Overall Beam: 467.1 meters
 Overall Draft: 140.5 meters
Displacement; 3, 309,000 metric tons
Crew Complement; 750 persons (varies)
Velocity:
 Cruising: Warp Factor 6
 Maximum: Warp Factor 9.6
Acceleration:
 Rest-Onset Critical Momentum: 11.06 sec
 Onset Critical Momentum-Warp Engage: 0.39 sec
 Warp 1-Warp 4: 0.72 sec
 Warp 4-Warp 6: 0.62 sec
 Warp 6-Warp 9.6: 2.63 sec
Duration:
 Standard Mission: 5 years
 Recommended Yard Overhaul: 20 years

Propulsion Systems:
 Warp: (2) LF-41 Advanced Linear Warp Drive Units
 Impulse: (2) FIG-5 Subatomic Unified Energy Impulse Units
Primary Computer System: M-15 Isolinear III Processor
Primary Navigation System: RAV/ISHAK Mod 3 Warp
 Celestial Guidance
Weapons:
 5 Type X Collimated Phaser Arrays
 3 Mk 80 Direct-Fire Photon Torpedo Tubes
Deflector Systems:
 CIDSS-3 Primary Force Field and Deflector Control System
Embarked Craft (Typical):
 4 Work Bee General Utility Craft
 12 Shuttlecraft (various classes)
 6 Shuttlepods (various classes)

U.S.S. ENTERPRISE NCC-1701-D

GALAXY-CLASS   FIRST COMMISSIONED: 2357

MISSION

Created to take deep-space exploration to a level never before attempted by Starfleet, the *Galaxy*-class starship was a radical departure in starship design. The ability to travel on missions of a decade or more in duration would give the *Galaxy*-class starships opportunities to explore farther into the reaches of space than ever before. The mission directives of the *Galaxy*-class included the following:

- Bring the cutting edge of Federation technology to both scientific and cultural research
- Become *the* primary instrument of exploration
- Execute Federation policy autonomously in outlying sectors
- Use any recent advancements on-site and to-the-moment to upgrade warp power-plant technology and improved science instrumentation

FEATURES

The *Galaxy*-class starship was not so much a breakthrough in technology as an innovative and cutting-edge combination of existing technologies into an ambitious starship design. Indeed, a great deal of the basic technology aboard the *Galaxy*-class starships had been utilized within the Federation for a number of decades. But the inspired application of those technologies within the *Galaxy*-class vessels clearly increased all levels of achievement.

Galaxy-class starships were among the earliest vessels to utilize routine hull-separation capabilities. Equipped with the first expanded quarters intended specifically to support civilians, the *Galaxy*-class personnel complement included families and children. Extensive holodeck facilities and family-style quarters made this a coveted post.

BACKGROUND

The *Galaxy*-class starship holds the rather dubious distinction of having had the longest design, development, and construction period of any class in Starfleet history. The design for the *Galaxy*-class was first developed in 2343, and the *U.S.S. Galaxy* herself left spacedock in 2357, followed by the *U.S.S. Yamato* and *U.S.S. Enterprise* in 2363.

Although a dozen spaceframes were assembled for construction into *Galaxy*-class starships, only six vessels were initially completed. The remaining frames were broken down, split apart, and concealed in key areas of the Federation to be assembled in time of emergency. That emergency came in 2366-2367, when the Borg arrived in Federation space and annihilated an entire Starfleet squadron sent to intercept them at Wolf 359. The Borg ship was ultimately stopped after reaching Earth orbit by the actions of the *Enterprise*. This crisis precipitated a major change in Starfleet's planning, which included the development of the *Defiant*-class and the *Akira*-class, as well as the construction of the second set of six *Galaxy*-class starships, which were built to upgraded specifications.

To date, three *Galaxy*-class vessels have been lost: the *Yamato*, the *Enterprise*, and the *Odyssey*. Superseded by the newer *Sovereign*-class, there are no plans, at the current time, to construct additional vessels of the *Galaxy*-class.

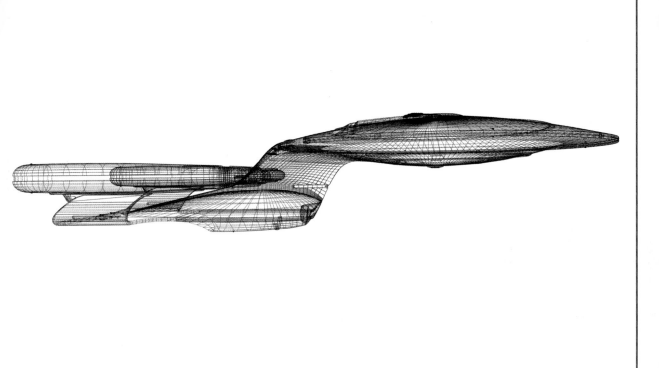

SPECIFICATIONS

Dimensions:
  Overall Length: 641 meters
  Overall Beam: 467.1 meters
  Overall Draft: 137.5 meters
Displacement: 4,500,000 metric tons
Crew Complement: 1,012 persons (varies)
Velocity:
  Cruising: Warp Factor 6
  Maximum: Warp Factor 9.6
Acceleration:
  Rest-Onset Critical Momentum: 12.04 sec
  Onset Critical Momentum-Warp Engage: 0.45 sec
  Warp 1-Warp 4: 0.68 sec
  Warp 4-Warp 6: 0.42 sec
  Warp 6-Warp 9.6: 3.76 sec
Duration:
  Standard Mission: 7 years
  Recommended Yard Overhaul: 20 years

Propulsion Systems:
  Warp: (2) LF-41 Advanced Linear Warp Drive Units
  Impulse: (3) FIG-5 Subatomic Unified Energy Impulse Units,
    (1 in stardrive, 2 in saucer)
Weapons:
  11 Type X Collimated Phaser Arrays
  3 Mk 80 Direct-Fire Photon Torpedo Tubes
Primary Computer System: M-15 Duotronic V Processor
Primary Navigation System: RAV/ISHAK Mod 3 Warp
  Celestial Guidance
Deflector Systems: CIDSS-3 Primary Force Field and Deflector
  Control System
Embarked Craft (Typical):
  4 Work Bee General Utility Craft
  8 Shuttlecraft (various classes)
  8 Shuttlepods (various classes)
  1 Captain's Yacht (Mark 1)

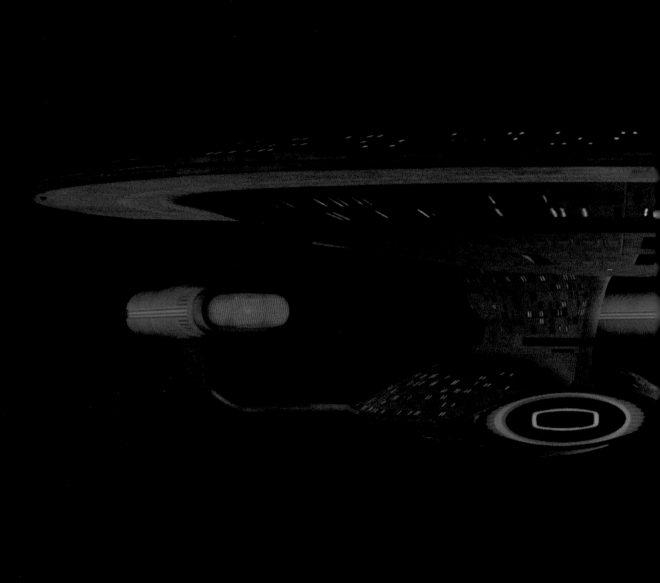

U.S.S. RIO GRANDE NCC-72452

DANUBE-CLASS RUNABOUT   FIRST COMMISSIONED: 2368

MISSION

Smaller than most starships yet larger than a Starfleet shuttlecraft, the *Danube*-class runabout fills an important role in Starfleet. The *Danube*-class was the outgrowth of a series of studies begun by the Advanced Starship Design Bureau (ASDB) in 2363 for a small, versatile vessel that could perform a series of short-term support missions in the areas of scientific research, personnel transfer, and vessel/facility resupply. While still technically a starship in designation and not a shuttlecraft (hence the application of "U.S.S." and the assignment of an individual NCC registry to each runabout), the *Danube*-class could supplement the fleet for certain specialized tasks. Several previous starship concepts went into the design of the *Danube*-class runabout with the goal of creating Starfleet's most refined and cutting-edge vessel to support a focused, limited-duration mission. The specific mission objectives of the *Danube*-class runabout include:

- Rapid-response scientific expedition transportation
- Orbital or landed base for science/research missions
- Transport for experiment and cargo modules
- Emergency and tactical mission support

The mission objective would only be limited by onboard supplies of fuel, weapons, and consumables.

FEATURES

The impressive versatility of the *Danube*-class runabout stems from its unique multimission pack, an interchangeable element that can be swapped out of the vessel and replaced as needed. Mounted amidships between the propulsion assemblies, this modular feature truly sets the *Danube*-class runabout apart from earlier designs. With four different module options available, mission specialists have a choice of a full swappable bay, a lateral half-bay, a longitudinal half-bay, or a one-quarter bay. The vessel can be configured to support a wide range and variety of mission parameters. Another unique feature of the *Danube*-class runabout is a cockpit section that can detach in an emergency situation and either operate in space (in a limited capacity) or make planetfall. Microtorpedo launchers augment the ship's defensive systems. Additional specialized strap-on equipment pods are available for mission-specific objectives, including pods customized for communications, ECM (electronic countermeasures), phasers, photon torpedoes, and sensors.

BACKGROUND

Initial flight trials for the *Danube*-class runabout proved so successful that active production of this design began immediately upon trial completion. Entering active service in 2368, the runabouts from the initial production run were assigned to Space Station Deep Space 9, in the Bajoran sector. These early runabouts quickly distinguished themselves in a series of high-profile missions, perhaps the most notable of which was the first contact with the Bajoran wormhole aliens. Interestingly, over more than a seven-year period, only one runabout out of the station's complement of four has continued in service: the *U.S.S. Rio Grande* NCC-74252. All of the other DS9 runabouts, from this delivery and several replacements, were either severely damaged or destroyed. There does not seem to be any specific factor that might explain this curious distinction. Still, it is worth noting.

Production on the *Danube*-class is continuing, even as Starfleet explores possible successor designs. The Utopia Planitia Yards serve as the primary runabout construction facility.

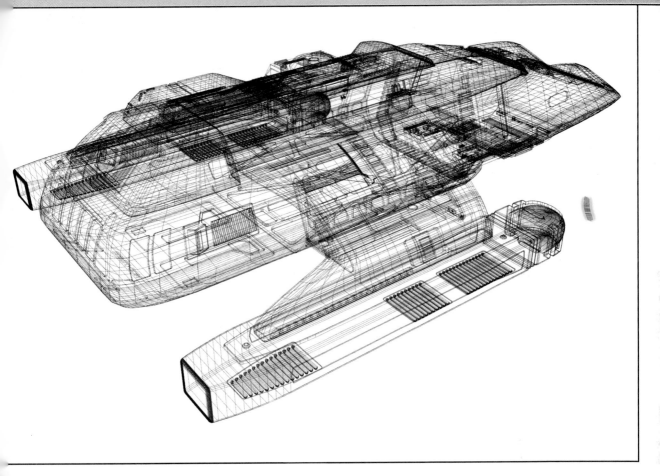

SPECIFICATIONS (BASIC CONFIGURATION)

Dimensions:
  Overall Length: 23.1 meters
  Overall Beam: 13.7 meters
  Overall Draft: 5.4 meters
Displacement: 158.7 metric tons
Crew Complement: 1 person (pilot) plus additional comple-
  ment as required
Velocity:
  Cruising: Warp Factor 4
  Maximum: Warp Factor 8.3
Acceleration:
  Rest-Onset Critical Momentum: 8.62 sec
  Onset Critical Momentum-Warp Engage: 1.03 sec
  Warp 1-Warp 4: 3.16 sec
  Warp 4-Warp 6: 2.14 sec
  Warp 6-Warp 8.3: 7.19 sec

Duration:
  Standard Mission: 1-2 weeks
  Recommended Yard Overhaul: 15 months
Propulsion Systems:
  Warp: (2)LF-7X2 Advanced Compact Linear Warp Drive Units
  Impulse: (2)FIB-3 Compact Subatomic Unified Energy
    Impulse Units
Weapons:
  6 Type VI Collimated Phaser Arrays
  2 Mk25 Direct-Fire Photon Microtorpedo Tubes
Primary Computer System: M-15 Isolinear III Processor
Primary Navigation System: RAV/ISHAK Mod 3 Warp
  Celestial Guidance
Deflector Systems: FSQ-2 Primary Force Field and Deflector
  Control System

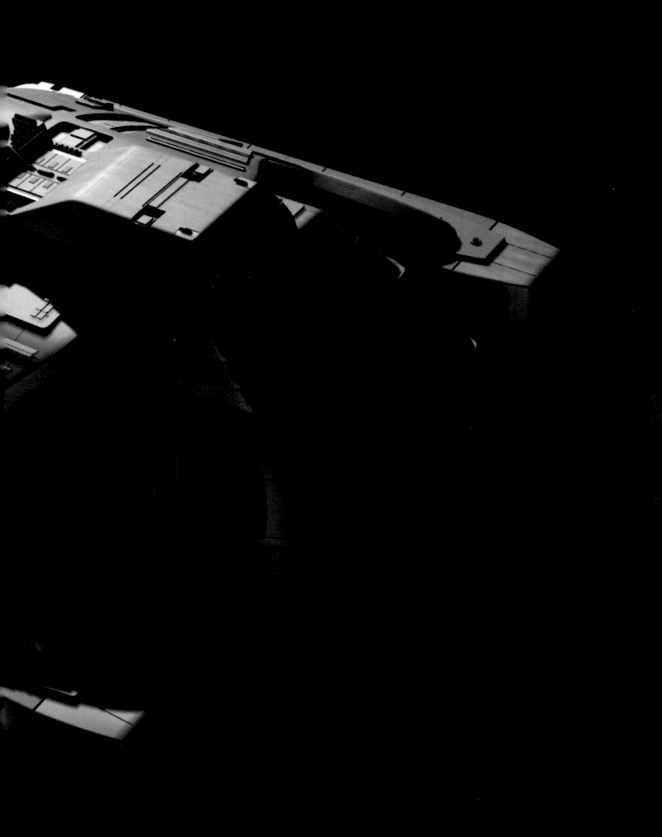

U.S.S. EQUINOX NCC-72381

NOVA-CLASS   FIRST COMMISSIONED: 2368

MISSION

Designed for short-range, limited duration missions of a research-oriented nature, the *Nova*-class starship has proven itself a useful instrument in furthering Starfleet's mission of scientific discovery. Planetary and/or system surveys of brief duration, weeks or months—in interior sectors of the Federation—comprise the primary mission profile for this ship. Generally, after the larger starships have passed through a given sector, smaller vessels like the *Nova*-class follow, doing extensive and in-depth research and analysis.

FEATURES

Large sensor arrays are the most noticeable characteristic of the *Nova*-class, and define it visually. The *Nova*-class is, essentially, a flying sensor platform. The vessel's finely tuned and integrated sensor suite allows research and analysis to a level unparalleled in Starfleet history.

Augmenting this sensing capability are two additional features that extend the ship's capabilities. First, the *Nova*-class is one of a series of smaller Starfleet vessels that have landing capability. Once almost unheard of in a Federation starship, the ability to set the craft down on a planetary surface has been made possible by breakthroughs in gravity control and vessel structural integrity. While not a routine operation, planetfall is now something that can be considered as part of a ship's mission, rather than an emergency response protocol. The second is the Waverider atmospheric operations shuttlecraft (AOS). Mounted in a specially designed port on the underside of the primary hull and able to reach one-half impulse, the Waverider is Starfleet's most advanced atmospheric craft.

BACKGROUND

The *Nova*-class is the successor to the long-lived *Oberth*-class ship. First commissioned in 2290, the *Oberth*-class saw extensive use over the years. But by 2365, this reliable ship was showing its age, and Starfleet began work on a successor.

The original *Defiant*-class pathfinder design was intended as a fast torpedo ship. But with the looming threat of the Borg, the entire *Defiant* concept was radically altered. This left Starfleet with an unapplied spaceframe that had performed extremely well in early warp-field simulations. The Advanced Starship Design Bureau (ASDB) then selected this promising design as a suitable basis for the new *Nova*-class ship. The pathfinder prototype underwent a large number of modifications, most notably the removal of the torpedo tubes and their replacement with powerful sensor arrays.

The *Nova*-class program hit one misstep very early on, when the *U.S.S. Equinox* vanished near the Badlands in 2370, shortly after its commissioning. As with any new class of vessel, the unexplained loss of a starship early in its service life became cause for great concern over the design. However, initial fears of a major design failure were set aside after a detailed analysis of the *U.S.S. Nova* revealed no discernible flaws. A few years later, when the *Equinox* was discovered in the Delta Quadrant by the *U.S.S. Voyager*, it turned out that the science ship had survived in conditions far above its design parameters. Although the *Equinox* was lost, the effectiveness of the design was thoroughly proven. Other vessels of the class, although not having experienced the rigors to which the *Equinox* had been subjected, have performed extremely well, leading Starfleet to step up production, confident that the *Nova*-class will effectively succeed the *Oberth*-class.

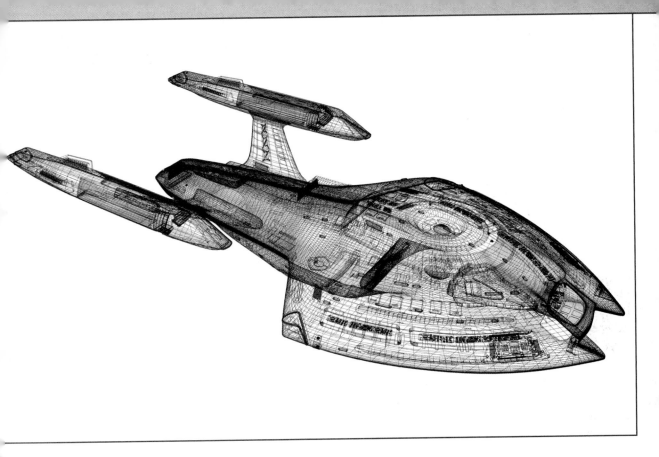

SPECIFICATIONS

Dimensions:
  Overall Length: 165 meters
  Overall Beam: 81.2 meters
  Overall Draft: 31.4 meters
Displacement: 110,000 metric tons
Crew Complement: 80 persons
Velocity:
  Cruising: Warp Factor 6
  Maximum: Warp Factor 8
Acceleration:
  Rest-Onset Critical Momentum: 7.84 sec
  Onset Critical Momentum-Warp Engage: 0.63 sec
  Warp 1-Warp 4: 0.95 sec
  Warp 4-Warp 6: 0.84 sec
  Warp 6-Warp 8: 4.09 sec
Duration:
  Standard Mission: 2 years
  Recommended Yard Overhaul: 7 years

Propulsion Systems:
  Warp: (2) LF-47 Advanced Linear Warp Drive Units
  Impulse: (2) FIG-7 Subatomic Unified Energy Impulse Units
Primary Computer System: M-15 Isolinear III Processor
Primary Navigation System: RAV/ISHAK Mod 3 Warp
  Celestial Guidance
Weapons:
  11 Type X Collimated Phaser Arrays
  2 Mk 95 Direct-Fire Photon Torpedo Tubes
Deflector Systems: FSQ Primary Force Field and Deflector
  Control System
Embarked Craft (Typical):
  2 Work Bee General Utility Craft
  2 Shuttlecraft (various classes)
  1 Waverider Atmospheric Operations Shuttle

U.S.S THUNDERCHILD NCC-63549

AKIRA-CLASS   FIRST COMMISSIONED: 2368

MISSION

Designed to supplement tactical support, the *Akira*-class starship fills the niche for a newer, capable combat-oriented vessel. The first cla of starship in several decades to rely heavily on torpedoes as primary armament, the *Akira*-class possesses substantial defensive power. Tl tactical mission elements of this ship allow for wider planetary support activities.

FEATURES

Taking its design cues from a "gunship," the *Akira*-class was the first vessel of this type to be widely produced by Starfleet. The *Akira*-class multiple tubes allow a potentially overwhelming strike from moderate range. The six phaser arrays are effective but act merely as a supple ment to the primary defense systems of the *Akira*-class.

In its role as a support ship, *Akira*-class has three quick pressure shuttle bays. A forward bay located at the bow of the starship utilize a three-tiered force field designed to allow for rapid deployment of shuttles or fighters. Two aft bays, mounted below and between th catamarans at the aft of the primary hull, are designed to facilitate a protected recovery of small craft. With such an extensive suppor capability, the *Akira*-class has become an extremely useful ship in a variety of missions.

BACKGROUND

Initially conceived during the buildup of hostilities with the Cardassian Union, the *Akira*-class starship didn't fully come to fruition until a decade later. Originally serving as a testbed ship for improving phasers and torpedoes, the ship was seen as purely an R&D vessel, never mean for wide-scale production. The Corp of Engineers worked on the design as a low-priority background project, an exercise more in ship design then anything else. The disastrous defeat and decimation of an entire Starfleet squadron at Wolf 359 by a single Borg cube shook th Federation. Starfleet undertook the building of several vessels to meet this threat, including the *Akira*-class. By 2368, the *U.S.S. Akira* wa launched. *Akira*-class ships distinguished themselves during the Dominion War, and are now part of Starfleet's defense forces.

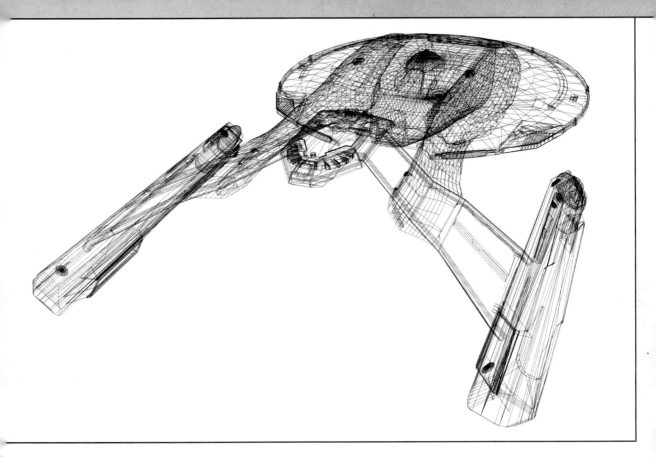

SPECIFICATIONS

Dimensions:
   Overall Length: 464.4 meters
   Overall Beam: 316.7 meters
   Overall Draft: 87.4 meters
Displacement: 3,055,000 metric tons
Crew Complement: 500 persons
Velocity:
   Cruising: Warp Factor 6
   Maximum: Warp Factor 9.8
Acceleration:
   Rest-Onset Critical Momentum: 5.48 sec
   Onset Critical Momentum-Warp Engage: 0.67 sec
   Warp 1-Warp 4: 0.84 sec
   Warp 4-Warp 6: 0.79 sec
   Warp 6-Warp 9.8: 5.03 sec
Duration:
   Standard Mission: 3 years
   Recommended Yard Overhaul: 18 years

Propulsion Systems:
   Warp: (2) LF-35 Advanced Linear Warp Drive Units
   Impulse: (2) FIG-5 Subatomic Unified Energy Impulse Units
              (2) FIG-4 Subatomic Unified Energy Impulse Units
Weapons:
   6 Type X Collimated Phaser Arrays
   15 Mk 80 Direct-Fire Photon Torpedo Tubes
Primary Computer System: M-14 Isolinear II Processor
Primary Navigation System: RAV/ISHAK Mod 2 Warp
   Celestial Guidance
Deflector Systems: FSQ-7 Primary Force Field and
   Deflector Control System
Embarked Craft (Typical):
   10 Work Bee General Utility Craft
   40 Fighters (various classes)
   10 Shuttlecraft (various classes)
   5 Shuttlepods (various classes)

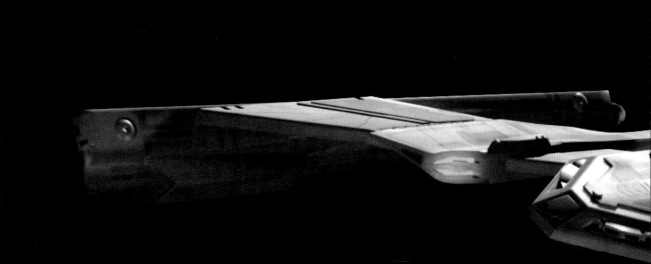

U.S.S. DEFIANT NX-74205

DEFIANT-CLASS   FIRST COMMISSIONED: 2370

MISSION

The *Defiant*-class was specifically designed to be a fast-attack craft, the first pure warship that Starfleet had ever created. Even in its earliest incarnations, *Defiant*'s primary mission objectives were to achieve high-warp penetration of enemy defenses. Starfleet engineers modified the vessel in the design phase to become a mobile defensive platform, with the ability to engage hostile forces and conduct covert operations.

FEATURES

Throughout its development phase, the *Defiant* prototype had been *the* testbed of some of the most advanced technologies available. Among its most notable elements, the *Defiant* featured a highly compact spaceframe with the nacelles in cowlings directly attached to the main hull, pulse phaser cannons, photon/quantum torpedo tubes, ablative armor plating, and a cloaking device provided by the Romulan government under a special amendment to the Treaty of Algeron. The *Defiant* prototype also contained advanced sensor systems. The warp core is a highly compact unit capable of delivering energy to meet the needs of a starship four times the *Defiant*'s size. Indeed, *Defiant*'s warp core rarely functioned at full capacity, because it was discovered that doing so endangered structural integrity. It wasn't until extensive field analysis and on-site development, by Commander Benjamin Sisko and Chief Miles O'Brien, had been conducted that the ship's propulsion and power systems could be run at design specifications.

BACKGROUND

From the very beginning, the *Defiant* prototype's development was intended to supplement Starfleet's tactical capability. The ship was initially conceived as a "Borg-buster," a response to the Borg threat. However, as time went on and a Borg invasion did not materialize, work on the *Defiant* slowed, leaving the ship to spend most of its time in spacedock at the Utopia Planitia Fleet Yards.

In late 2371, following the initial contact with the Dominion, the *Defiant* prototype was deployed to Deep Space 9. Her mission was to defend the station from attack. It was at this time that the vessel was fitted with a Romulan cloaking device. The Treaty of Algeron forbade the Federation from developing cloaking technology. However, the Romulans perceived the Dominion as a threat to the entire Alpha Quadrant. They felt it wiser to allow a Starfleet ship to gather critical intelligence with a cloaking device, rather than commit the resources of the Romulan Empire.

A number of system adjustments and developmental upgrades were implemented to the *Defiant* prototype. Vessel performance improved, and further analysis showed that the remaining problems were readily correctable. As the Dominion threat began to build, Starfleet Command ordered the *Defiant*-class into full production. By the time the situation had escalated into full-scale warfare, several *Defiant*-class vessels were already operational. The *U.S.S. Defiant* herself performed admirably in a variety of missions, but fell victim to a Breen energy dampening weapon in 2375, and was destroyed. Another *Defiant*-class vessel, the *U.S.S. Sao Paulo*, was assigned to Deep Space 9 as a replacement. A special dispensation was made by Starfleet Command for the ship to be renamed *Defiant*, and to retain its original registry number.

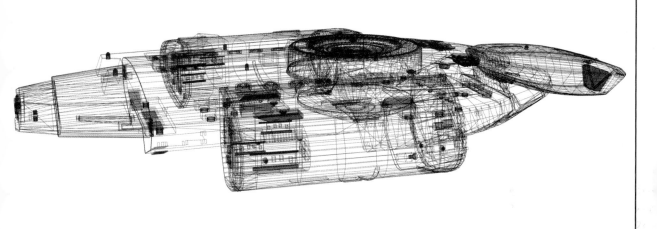

SPECIFICATIONS

Dimensions:
   Overall Length: 119.5 meters
   Overall Beam: 90.3 meters
   Overall Draft: 25.5 meters
Displacement: 355,000 metric tons
Crew Complement: 40 persons
Velocity:
   Cruising: Warp Factor 6
   Maximum: Warp Factor 9.982
Acceleration:
   Rest-Onset Critical Momentum: 3.92 sec
   Onset Critical Momentum-Warp Engage: 0.48 sec
   Warp 1-Warp 4: 0.96 sec
   Warp 4-Warp 6: 2.81 sec
   Warp 4-Warp 9.982: 4.12 sec
Duration:
   Standard Mission: 2 years
   Recommended Yard Overhaul: 12 years

Propulsion Systems:
   Warp: (2) LF-35 Advanced Linear Warp Drive Units
   Impulse: (2) FIG-2 Subatomic Unified Energy Impulse Units
Weapons:
   4 Type XII Pulse Phaser Cannons
   2 Mk 75 Direct-Fire Photon/Quantum Torpedo Tubes
Primary Computer System: M-15 Isolinear III Processor
Primary Navigation System: RAV/ISHAK Mod 3 Warp
   Celestial Guidance
Deflector Systems: FSQ Primary Force Field and Deflector
   Control System
Embarked Craft (Typical):
   1 Shuttlecraft (Type-10)
   4 Shuttlepods (various classes)

SHUTTLECRAFT CHAFFEE

TYPE-10-CLASS SHUTTLECRAFT   FIRST COMMISSIONED: 2373

MISSION

The cutting-edge Type-10 class marks one of those rare instances in Starfleet history that a shuttlecraft has been designed primarily for military purposes. Starfleet shuttles do come equipped with limited defensive systems; however, their primary mission profile does not typically involve combat, but rather short-range personnel transfers, planetary ops, limited deep space scouting and reconnaissance, and emergency starship escape. The Type-10 class, while sharing these mission-specific capabilities, comes equipped with more powerful weapons and larger warp coil assemblies for increased speed, and is more heavily shielded. The Type-10-class shuttlecraft can also act in a tactical assistance role during combat, and provide a stronger defense for escape pods in the event a starship is damaged or destroyed.

FEATURES

Building on the lessons learned from successful modifications to the *Defiant*-class, the Type-10-class shuttlecraft shares many similar systems with its "big sister" starship. The Type-10 shuttle's most noticeable *Defiant*-inspired feature is its recessed, armored engine pods. No longer situated away from the hull on potentially vulnerable support pylons, the Type-10's protected engines eliminate a tactical weakness. Based on a Type-6 shuttle spaceframe design, the insides of the Type-10 more closely resemble those of a starship. Subscale versions of starship warp and impulse propulsion systems give the Type-10 shuttlecraft an impressive capacity for speed. Weapons systems include standard phaser arrays, but also feature the capability to launch modified quantum torpedoes through micro-torpedo launchers. Onboard computer systems are based on a shortened version of the computer core utilized by the *Danube*-class runabout. Successful field tests of the *Intrepid* class have stepped up the targeted system upgrade of Type-10 shuttlecraft to a bio-neural gelpack computer system.

BACKGROUND

In 2370, when the *Galaxy*-class starship *U.S.S. Odyssey* (NCC-71832) was destroyed by Jem'Hadar attack ships, Starfleet revisited several starship designs. Already prototyped, the new *Defiant*-class was added to the production schedule. After more than eighteen months of practical and mission-specific upgrades, the *Defiant*'s design had reached a point where Starfleet felt confident bringing the class into active service. The Corp of Engineers felt that additional shuttlecraft support was needed.

A small starship footprint, the *Defiant* included room for only four shuttlepods with capabilities limited to planetary ops, ship-to-ship transfers, and starship escape. Fortunately, the *Defiant*-class had an underused area on Decks 3 and 4, just below the bridge. This space was intended for future computer and weapons system upgrades. Instead it was converted into a second shuttle bay capable of housing a single Type-10 shuttlecraft. Beginning in 2372, system components were developed for the Type-10 in parallel with the construction of design upgrades of the *Defiant*-class. As new *Defiant*-class ships were launched, they were immediately equipped with their own Type-10 shuttlecraft. Other *Defiant*-class ships already in service were retrofitted.

With the cessation of hostilities between the Dominion and the Federation in 2375, Starfleet started a re-evaluation of the performance of the Type-10 shuttlecraft, both as a support craft for the *Defiant*-class and in other service areas throughout the fleet.

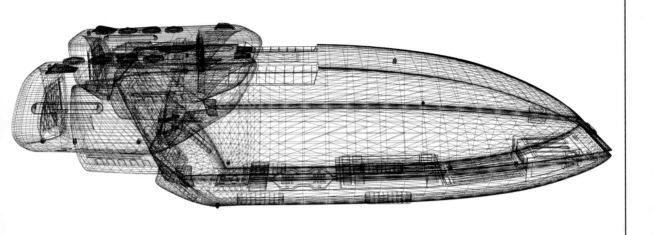

SPECIFICATIONS

Dimensions:
    Overall Length: 9.64 meters
    Overall Beam: 5.82 meters
    Overall Draft: 3.35 meters
Displacement: 19.73 metric tons
Crew Complement: 4 persons
Velocity:
    Cruising: Warp Factor 3
    Maximum: Warp Factor 5
Acceleration:
    Rest-Onset Critical Momentum: 12.03 sec
    Onset Critical Momentum-Warp Engage: 0.64 sec
    Warp 1-Warp 3: 1.53 sec
    Warp 3-Warp 5: 6.97 sec

Duration:
    Standard Mission: 1 week
    Recommended Yard Overhaul: 18 months
Propulsion Systems:
    Warp: (2) LF-6 Advanced Compact Linear Warp Drive Units
    Impulse: (2) FIA Compact Subatomic Unified Energy
        Impulse Units
Weapons:
    2 Type V Collimator Phaser Arrays
    2 Mk 25 Direct-Fire Photon/Quantum Torpedo Tubes
Primary Computer System: M-15 Isolinear III Processor
Primary Navigation System: RAV/ISHAK Mod 3C Warp
    Celestial Guidance
Deflector Systems: FSQ-1A Primary Force Field and
    Deflector Control System

U.S.S. VOYAGER NCC-74656

INTREPID-CLASS   FIRST COMMISSIONED: 2370

MISSION

The *Intrepid*-class starship marks a change in course for Starfleet away from building very large, elaborate starships and toward build smaller, more efficient vessels. One of a series of newer and more compact ships, the *Intrepid*-class was designed to be a fast multimissi starship primarily intended for exploration, survey, and courier missions. A fast vessel with advanced sensing and research capability, *Intrepid*-class makes for an effective exploratory platform, while at the same time carrying sufficient armament to act as an interdiction a combat vessel.

FEATURES

Several important advances in Starfleet technology mark the development of the *Intrepid*-class. One of the most important features this starship is the variable geometry warp nacelles, which allow an adjustment of the warp field to maximize its efficiency, as well as to mi imize any negative effects on the fabric of space. Utilizing this cutting-edge technology results in a vessel that can be flown at extreme high speeds with a significantly smaller power source than other ships of comparable size. Another design breakthrough in the *Intrepid*-cl is the inclusion within a protected backup chamber of a series of components that would allow for the assembly of a spare warp core. Shou the main core be lost for some unforeseen reason, a replacement could be constructed by the engineering crew without having to replica all the components.

The *Intrepid*-class pioneered the systems that would allow a starship to make routine planetfall. Previously unheard of in starships, the ab ity to land and take off again with minimum system impact is being incorporated into a series of vessels, thanks in large part to the advanc made and lessons learned in the flight of the *Intrepid*-class.

The most advanced computer systems available are at the heart of the *Intrepid*-class ship. The computer uses bio-neural gelpacks th incorporate synthetic neuron-analogs in a nutrient gel medium. This arrangement mimics organic neurons, allowing the packs a processin protocol akin to what happens in a humanoid brain, speeding data functions and improving overall computer operations.

BACKGROUND

After an initial order of four *Intrepid*-class starships was approved, the first ships, *U.S.S. Intrepid* and *U.S.S. Voyager,* left space dock Utopia Planitia at the end of 2370 and beginning of 2371, respectively. On its first-ever mission, the *U.S.S. Voyager* vanished early in 2371 the Badlands, an area of space known for its hostile natural environment. At first, Starfleet Command believed the *Voyager* was not a victi of castastrophic system failure, rather it was believed to have been a casualty of plasma storms or the victim of the Maquis. Other *Intrepic* class starships proved themselves extremely effective and reliable, and rapidly secured their niche in the fleet.

It was not until several years later that Starfleet learned *Voyager* was still intact and operational. It had been transported to the far reach es of the Delta Quadrant, some seventy-thousand light-years from Sector 001. The *U.S.S. Voyager* and her crew, by the time their odyssey wa done, had survived multiple encounters with the Borg and logged more first contacts than any Federation starship. The ship finally returne to Earth in 2377. The starship's logs provided extensive and invaluable data on the operation of the *Intrepid*-class in an unsupported env ronment, and this data was immediately poured into the development of the next round of upgrades and refits for the class.

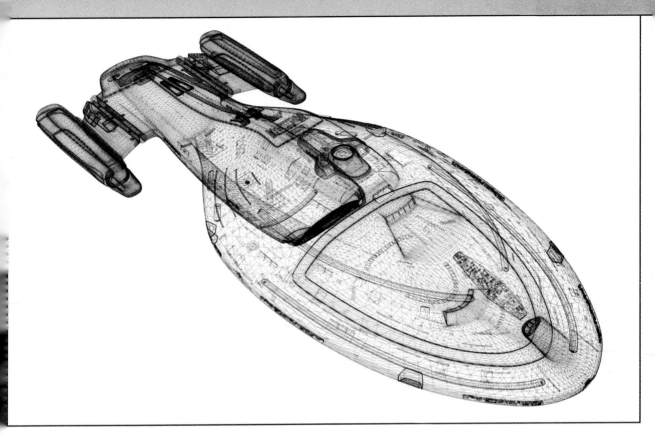

SPECIFICATIONS (2270)

Dimensions:
  Overall Length: 344.5 meters
  Overall Beam: 132.1 meters
  Overall Draft: 64.4 meters
Displacement: 700,000 metric tons
Crew Complement: 150 persons
Velocity:
  Cruising: Warp Factor 6
  Maximum: Warp Factor 9.975
Acceleration:
  Rest-Onset Critical Momentum: 4.08 sec
  Onset Critical Momentum-Warp Engage: 0.59 sec
  Warp 1-Warp 4: 1.08 sec
  Warp 4-Warp 6: 2.91 sec
  Warp 6-Warp 9.975: 5.65 sec
Duration:
  Standard Mission: 6 years
  Recommended Yard Overhaul: 24 years

Propulsion Systems:
  Warp: (2) LF-45 Advanced Linear Warp Drive Units
  Impulse: (2) FIG-4 Subatomic Unified Energy Impulse Units
Weapons:
  11 Type X Collimated Phaser Arrays
  4 Mk 95 Direct-Fire Photon Torpedo Tubes
Primary Computer System: M-16 Bio-Neural Gelpack
  Isolinear III Processor
Primary Navigation System: RAV/ISHAK Mod 3 Warp
  Celestial Guidance
Deflector Systems: FSQ Primary Force Field and Deflector
  Control System
Embarked Craft (Typical):
  2 Workpods
  4 Shuttlecraft (various classes)
  2 Shuttlepods (various classes)
  1 Aeroshuttle Atmospheric Craft
  1 Delta Flyer (*Voyager* only)

AEROSHUTTLE

ATMOSPHERIC OPERATIONS CRAFT   FIRST COMMISSIONED: 2370

MISSION

Designed to support and enhance the exploration and survey abilities of the *Intrepid*-class starship, the aeroshuttle is a vehicle optimized for atmospheric flight. Its capabilities are similar to those of a *Danube*-class runabout, but the aeroshuttle is more focused on the kind of survey and support missions which require entry into and operations within planetary atmospheres. The aeroshuttle is structurally reinforced and able to operate effectively inside of a planetary atmosphere ranging from Class-D to Class-J. Not being modular, the aeroshuttle is less versatile than a runabout. However, this limitation is in keeping with the aeroshuttle's role as a support craft, rather than an independently operating small starship.

FEATURES

The aeroshuttle shares many systems with the *Danube*-class runabout, including thruster assemblies, the impulse drive, cockpit configuration, and weapons systems. While the runabout is a faster deep-space vessel, the streamlined hull and large reinforced wings of the aeroshuttle make it significantly more efficient in high-speed atmospheric maneuvers and operations. The aeroshuttle also comes equipped with a variety of sensor arrays for maximum data-gathering capability, particularly useful for planetary surveys. If needed the sensors can also be used for covert or reconnaissance operations.

BACKGROUND

Initially prototyped for use aboard the *Intrepid*-class starships, the aeroshuttle marked the first of a new breed of support craft, derived from the *Danube*-class runabouts. Larger than a typical Class-1 shuttlecraft, yet still slightly smaller than a standard runabout, the aeroshuttle presented a potential problem in that it would occupy an inefficiently large amount of shuttlebay space on a small starship like the *Intrepid*-class. So Starfleet engineers designed into the *Intrepid*-class a supplemental shuttlebay located beneath the primary saucer hull intended exclusively for the aeroshuttle. Similar in concept to the captain's yacht of the *Galaxy*-class and *Sovereign*-class, the aeroshuttle could be maintained in a separate area of the ship without impacting standard shuttlecraft operations.

Using off-the-shelf technologies and components, the aeroshuttles proved themselves as an innovative design that made them known as effective support craft. The success of the aeroshuttle led to the design of the more advanced Waverider shuttlecraft currently deployed aboard the *Nova*-class starships.

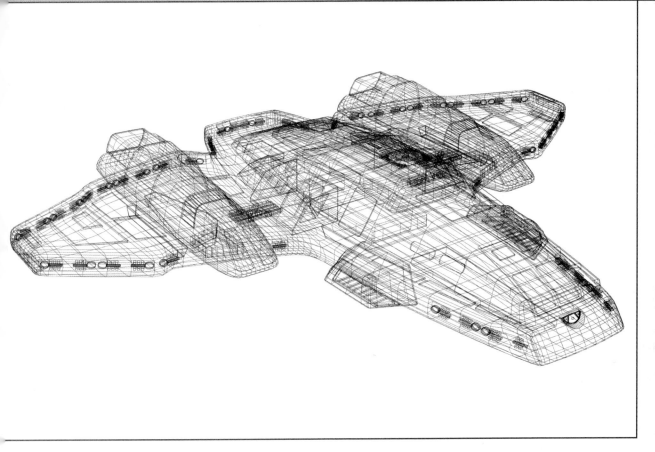

SPECIFICATIONS (BASIC CONFIGURATION)

Dimensions:
  Overall Length: 24.8 meters
  Overall Beam: 29.6 meters (full wingspan)
  Overall Draft: 4.1 meters
Displacement: 222.5 metric tons
Crew Complement: 1 pilot—5 crew
Velocity:
  Cruising: Warp Factor 3
  Maximum: Warp Factor 5
Acceleration:
  Rest-Onset Critical Momentum: 10.83 sec
  Onset Critical Momentum-Warp Engage: 1.47 sec
  Warp 1-Warp 3: 4.79 sec
  Warp 3-Warp 5: 6.51 sec
Duration:
  Standard Mission: 2 weeks
  Recommended Yard Overhaul: 18 months

Propulsion Systems:
  Warp: (2) LF-9X4 Advanced Compact Linear Warp Drive Units
  Impulse: (2) FIB-3 Compact Subatomic Unified
    Energy Impulse Units
Weapons:
  4 Type VI Collimated Phaser Arrays
  2 Mk 25 Direct-Fire Photon Microtorpedo Tubes
Primary Computer System: M-15 Isolinear III Processor
Primary Navigation System: RAV/ISHAK Mod 3 Warp
  Celestial Guidance
Deflector Systems: FSQ-2 Primary Force Field and Deflector
  Control System

SHUTTLECRAFT DELTA FLYER

DELTA FLYER-CLASS SHUTTLECRAFT   FIRST COMMISSIONED: 2375

MISSION

The brainchild of *U.S.S. Voyager* conn officer Lieutenant (jg) Thomas Paris, the *Delta Flyer* was an entirely new approach to a shuttlecraft. Lieutenant Paris initially conceived of the *Flyer* as a sort of deep space "hot rod." Paris envisioned a vehicle larger and more capable than the standard shuttlecraft that *Voyager* was carrying as part of its regular shuttle complement. The final design of the *Delta Flyer* reflected the enhanced, multimission capability that Paris sought, and the *Flyer* quickly became one of the most regularly used vehicles in *Voyager*'s small-craft inventory.

FEATURES

Substantially larger than a regular shuttlecraft, the *Delta Flyer* is nearly as large as a runabout. With a hull constructed of tetraburnium for enhanced structural strength, the *Delta Flyer* is warp capable, using a compact circumferential warp reactor. Like any standard shuttlecraft, the *Flyer* can operate in an atmosphere and is landing-capable. It also has a narrow-beam transporter. At the insistence of Lieutenant Paris, some of the flight controls were made to resemble panels from the holonovel *Captain Proton*. Paris's intention was to allow the pilot to "feel" the reactions of the craft as he manipulated the controls, something not generally possible using Starfleet's standard flat-panel console designs.

The weapons and shields on the *Delta Flyer* are heavily augmented with Borg technology, provided by Seven of Nine—a former drone now working as a member of *Voyager*'s crew. Finally, to further enhance the craft's adaptability, the aft section includes a hardpoint to which can be attached custom-designed mission modules, ranging from lab units to cargo pods.

BACKGROUND

Thousands of light-years away in the Delta Quandrant, *Voyager* faced numerous hostile situations that would have challenged any starship and crew. Numerous encounters with belligerent species and spatial/temporal anomalies resulted in significant damage to *Voyager* and the eventual loss of nearly two dozen shuttlecraft. Shortly before the construction of the *Delta Flyer*, *Voyager*'s Chief Engineer B'Elanna Torres commented, "If I have to rebuild one more shuttlecraft, I'm going to go space crazy."

Paris's initial suggestion to build a shuttlecraft better suited to the *Voyager*'s unique situation was not acted upon immediately. Resources were obviously limited onboard *Voyager*. However, after an initial period of resistance from Captain Janeway and Commander Chakotay, circumstances eventually led the entire senior staff to begin work on the ambitious construction project. The *Delta Flyer* performed well on its maiden flight: the retrieval of a probe from the atmosphere of a gas giant. It wasn't long before the *Delta Flyer* became *Voyager*'s most-used craft for away missions.

The original *Delta Flyer* was destroyed during an action against the Borg in 2376. However, the *Flyer*'s usefulness had long since been proven. A replacement *Delta Flyer* was constructed, which operated aboard *Voyager* throughout the rest of its journey back to the Alpha Quadrant.

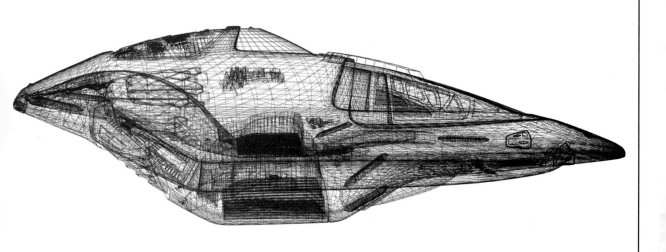

SPECIFICATIONS (BASIC CONFIGURATION)

Dimensions:
  Overall Length: 21 meters
  Overall Beam: 12.2 meters
  Overall Draft: 5.3 meters
Displacement: 180.6 metric tons
Crew Complement: 1 person (pilot)—additional complement as
  mission requirements dictate
Velocity:
  Cruising: Warp Factor 3
  Maximum: Warp Factor 6
Acceleration:
  Rest-Onset Critical Momentum: 13.08 sec
  Onset Critical Momentum-Warp Engage: 1.3 sec
  Warp 1-Warp 3: 4.79 sec
  Warp 3-Warp 6: 3.56 sec

Duration:
  Standard Mission: 10 days
  Recommended Yard Overhaul: 2 months
Propulsion Systems:
  Warp: (2) Tuned Circumferential Warp Drive Units
  Impulse: (2) Compact Subatomic Unified Energy
    Impulse Units
Weapons:
  8 Type V Collimated Phaser Arrays
  1 Mk 25 Direct-Fire Photon Microtorpedo Tube
Primary Computer System: Custom-Designed
  Isolinear III Processor
Primary Navigation System: Paris-1 Mod 1 Warp
  Celestial Guidance
Deflector Systems: Custom-Designed Primary Force Field
  and Deflector Control System

U.S.S. PROMETHEUS NX-59650

PROMETHEUS-CLASS   FIRST COMMISSIONED: 2374

MISSION

The *Prometheus*-class starship represents the most advanced, cutting-edge design concept in the fleet. A long-range ship intended to carry an offensive to the very doorstep of a hostile force, the *Prometheus* is a response to an increasing number of recent threats to the safety of the Federation. Designed to utilize the revolutionary "multivector assault mode," the *Prometheus* can deliver crushing force against a hostile threat during its attacks. In effect, the *Prometheus* can become three ships, each operating semi-independently and in concert with the other components.

FEATURES

The multivector assault mode is the most unique feature of the *U.S.S. Prometheus*. Tactically unique within Starfleet, this remarkable technological breakthrough allows the single starship to function as three separate spacecraft, outmaneuvering, and outflanking a larger hostile vessel. In order to support the complex systems, the *Prometheus* carries the most advanced computer systems currently available. This prototype vessel also boasts state-of-the-art control systems, an advanced sickbay, a shipwide holoemitter array, ablative armor hull plating, and regenerative shielding. The control systems are so advanced, a crew of as few as four persons can operate the ship from the bridge.

BACKGROUND

The *U.S.S. Prometheus* is undergoing a rigorous testing phase. The sheer complexity of its many systems requires an extended period of testing and re-testing to ensure that these systems work. The level of automation on the *Prometheus* is more substantial than any other starship control system since the early M-5 multitronic unit was tested on board the *U.S.S. Enterprise* NCC-1701 (2268). During her first deep-space testing, only four people were rated to operate the *Prometheus*.

The *Prometheus* became a target of military espionage. On its first field-testing run in 2374, a group of Romulan Tal Shiar agents attempted to hijack the *Prometheus* and take it into Romulan space. The attempt ended in failure. With the Starfleet crew murdered and the Romulans in control of the vessel, the Emergency Medical Hologram (EMH) of the *Prometheus* was activated by the EMH from the *Starship Voyager*. The *Voyager* EMH had been beamed to the *Prometheus* via an advanced alien relay system in an attempt to contact Starfleet. Together, the two EMHs regained control of the *Prometheus* and aided a Starfleet pursuit force in combat against several Romulan warbirds. Rescued but heavily damaged in the incident, the *Prometheus* was returned to the Beta Antares shipyards for repair. Testing has resumed, under significantly heightened security.

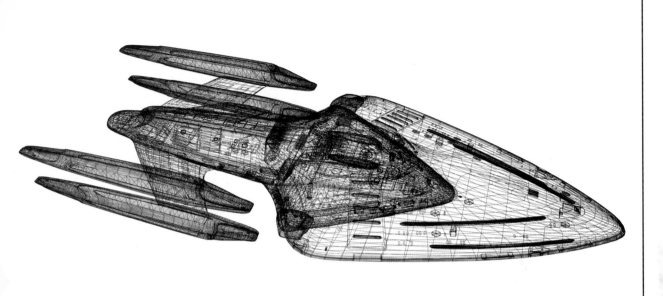

SPECIFICATIONS (MERGED CONFIGURATION)

Dimensions:
  Overall Length: 415 meters
  Overall Beam: 170 meters
  Overall Draft: 113 meters
Displacement: 850,000 metric tons
Crew Complement: 141 persons
Velocity:
  Cruising: Warp Factor 9
  Maximum: Warp Factor 9.99
Acceleration:
  Rest-Onset Critical Momentum: 4.12 sec
  Onset Critical Momentum-Warp Engage: 0.54 sec
  Warp 1-Warp 4: 0.63 sec
  Warp 4-Warp 7: 0.76 sec
  Warp 7-Warp 9.99: 5.08 sec
Duration:
  Standard Mission: 1 year
  Recommended Yard Overhaul: N/A

Propulsion Systems:
  Warp: (4) LF-50 Mod 1 Advanced Linear Warp Drive Units
          (1) LF-12X Mod 2 Compact Linear Warp Drive Unit
  Impulse: (3) FIG-5 Subatomic Unified Energy Impulse Units
Weapons:
  13 Type XII Collimated Phaser Arrays
  3 Mk 95 Direct-Fire Photon Torpedo Tubes
Primary Computer System: M-16 Bio-neural Gelpack
  Isolinear III Processor
Primary Navigation System: RAV/ISHAK Mod 3 Warp
  Celestial Guidance
Deflector Systems: FSS Primary Force Field and Deflector
  Control System
Embarked Craft (Typical):
  2 Shuttlecraft (various classes)
  4 Shuttlepods (various classes)

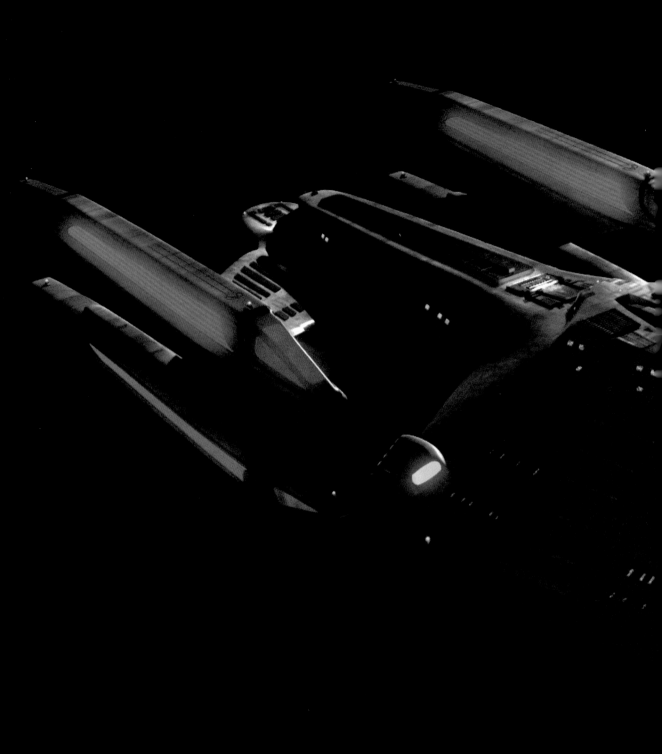

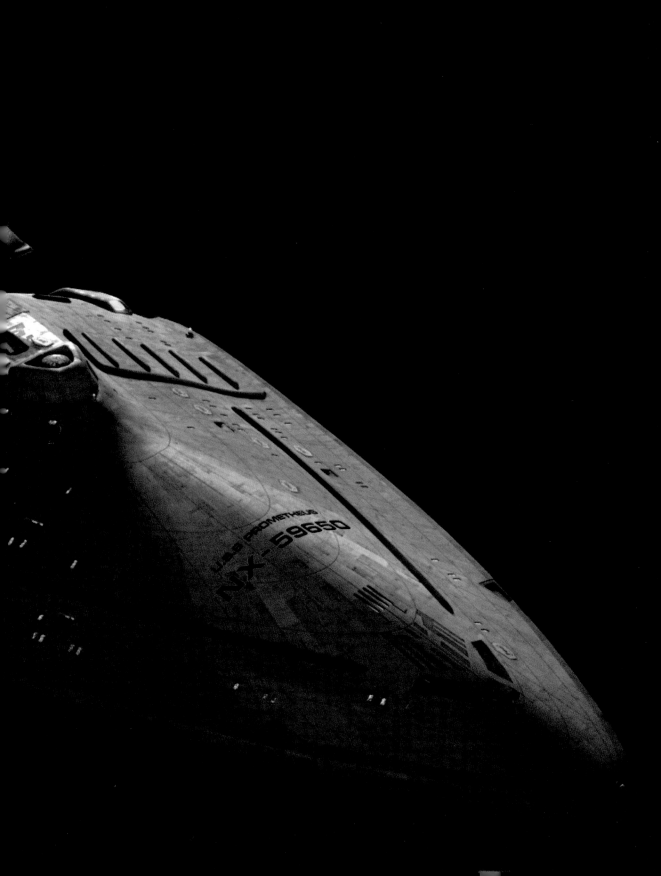

SPACEDOCK

FIRST COMMISSIONED: 2276

MISSION

Originally designed to support Starfleet operations in the Sol sector of space, spacedock is a huge, multipurpose facility serving in the role of forward base, industrial center, operations hub, shipyard, and research facility. More protected than open fleetyards spacedock also serve as a starship construction facility, as well as a key administrative nexus for Starfleet Command. The facility supports a large operation specialist base, and frequently is the first contact nonallied worlds have with the Federation.

FEATURES

A city in space, spacedock can support up to eight *Galaxy*-class vessels, and up to twenty-four smaller ships. Initially designed for the smaller starships of the twenty-third century, two of the station's spacedoors were enlarged in the mid-twenty-fourth century to accommodate the *Galaxy*-class starships. The giant sensor towers and the forest of antennae allow the facility to scan for light-years around the area of the station. Non-Starfleet endeavors are welcome at the spacedocks, retail and office space along with cargo holds are available. Starfleet provides transporter service and trade arbitration, if necessary. Many spacedocks also have a significant tourist trade, by virtue of its role as gateway to the sector it serves. Advanced medical and research facilities are found on many spacedocks. The only limit to a spacedock is the imagination of its commander.

BACKGROUND

The spacedock was first conceived during conflicts with the Klingon Empire. By the end of 2259, the facility had been approved. However design profiles were stalled for years as system upgrades were added. It was a long, slow process, as this was the largest contained space borne facility Starfleet had ever attempted to build. The first spacedock was completed in 2276 in the Sol sector.

The spacedock design worked so well that it became the standard within Starfleet. Although spacedock itself was not conceived as a starbase, it became one. Several starbases, in fact, were commissioned as an enlarged version of the spacedock design. By the late twenty-fourth century, the mushroom shape of the spacedock had become one of the most recognizable symbols of Starfleet.

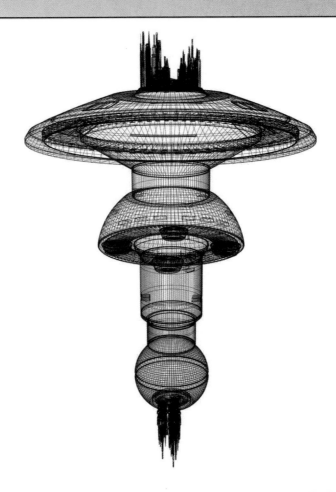

SPECIFICATIONS (CA. 2290)

Dimensions:
    Overall Length: 4,600 meters
    Overall Beam: 4,600 meters
    Overall Draft: 6,900-6,950 meters (depending on comm-
        tower configuration)
Displacement: 236,642,306 metric tons
Crew Complement: 76,625 persons (civilians and transients)
Velocity: N/A
Acceleration: N/A
Duration: Open-Ended
Propulsion Systems: N/A
Weapons:
    80 RIM-12C Independent Twin Mount Phaser
      Emplacements (40 banks/2 each)

Primary Computer System:
    Original Configuration: M-10 Duotronic IV Processor
    Current Configuration: M15A Bio-neural Gelpack
      Isolinear II-a Processor
Primary Navigation System: N/A
Deflector Systems: Primary Force Field and Deflector
    Control System
Embarked Craft (Typical):
    285 Work Bee Class General Utility Craft
    100 Shuttlecraft (various classes)
    50 *Danube*-class runabouts

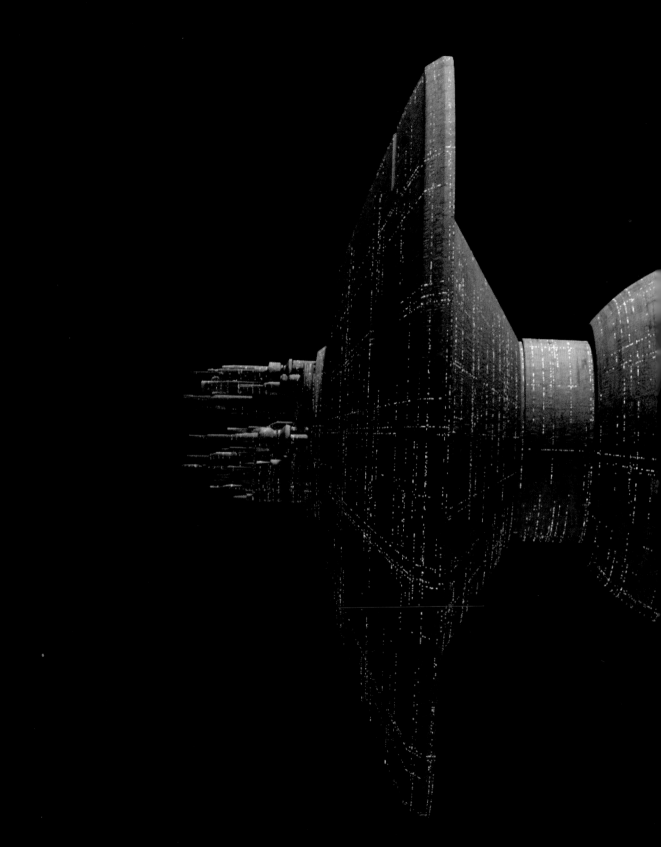

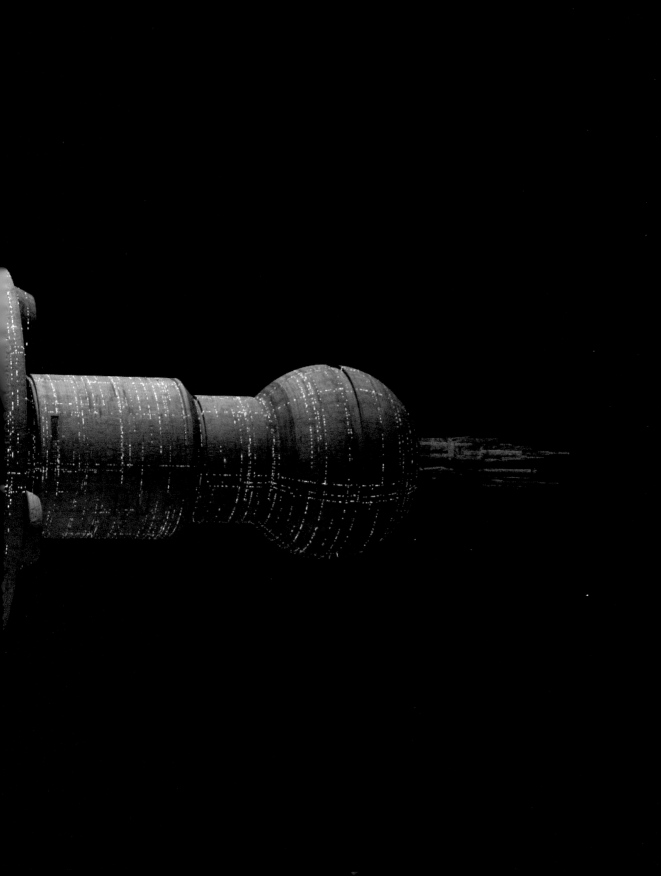

MIDAS ARRAY

STARFLEET COMMUNICATIONS AND REMOTE SENSING PLATFORM
FIRST CONSTRUCTED: 2367

MISSION

Designed as a deep space monitoring and scanning station, the mission profile of the MIDAS Array has evolved to include a unique function as a transgalactic communications relay. An acronym for the *Mutara Inter-dimensional Deep-space-transponder Array System*, MIDAS can transmit and receive signals across a wide band of both the electromagnetic and subspace spectra. Its primary function is as a long-range sensor, monitoring distant areas of the galaxy. As a transmitter, MIDAS Array has become a test platform for hyper-subspace communications and ultimately a conduit through which two-way signals can be sent via a microwormhole across nearly thirty-thousand light-years of space from the Alpha to the Delta Quadrant.

FEATURES

The MIDAS Array is one of Starfleet's most advanced communications and remote sensing instruments. Frequently upgraded with the latest long-range monitoring technology, the MIDAS Array can literally see across the galaxy. A successor to the extremely well known Argus Array, the MIDAS Array is more powerful. The MIDAS Array has the additional ability to transmit an incredibly powerful range of signals from a series of highly specialized graviton emitters directed through a unique control matrix focusing/receiving antenna. This antenna can be raised above the central receiving disk to amplify graviton and tachyon pulses beamed from the emitters. The emitters are also modular and can adjust their angle of displacement for extremely accurate targeting of emissions from the array. For additional power generation, the MIDAS Array is equipped with three highly efficient solar/rad collector arrays which can function as backup.

BACKGROUND

The Borg incursion of 2366 drove home the need for an early-warning long-range sensor and tracking system. While the Argus Array was a good start, Starfleet needed to see farther, faster. The MIDAS Array was conceived and quickly constructed. Ironically, by the time the Array was deployed, Starfleet had learned of the Borg's transwarp capabilities and the Array was outmoded. The Starfleet Communications Research Center endeavored to find practical applications for the Array's unique abilities.

Such an opportunity presented itself when Starfleet Command learned of the fate of the *Starship Voyager*, lost deep within the Delta Quadrant and trying to return home. Without the ability to contact the crew over such a great distance, Starfleet assembled its greatest engineering minds for the Pathfinder Project, a team dedicated to finding a way to communicate with *Voyager*. Working with a group of Vulcan scientists, an initial plan was conceived to create a hyper-subspace signal that could reach *Voyager* in a matter of days instead of months or years. Unfortunately, communication would be one-way only.

A breakthrough came thanks to the efforts of Lieutenant Reginald Barclay, who hypothesized that an artificial quantum singularity (a microwormhole) could be created by directing a tachyon beam from the MIDAS Array to a nearby Class-B itinerant pulsar. This microwormhole was then used to transmit a compressed datastream to and from *Voyager* once every thirty-two days—the periodic window of alignment for the pulsar. Later, by bouncing an additional tachyon beam off of both ends of the artificial singularity, the Pathfather Project was able to activate a transgalactic comm-link with *Voyager* for eleven minutes per day, with the starship at nearly thirty thousand light-years away.

Breakthroughs such as Barclay's and other advances achieved by the Pathfinder Project utilizing the Array hold great promise for ensuring future Starfleet exploratory vessels having the ability to communicate as they venture farther out into the vast reaches of space.

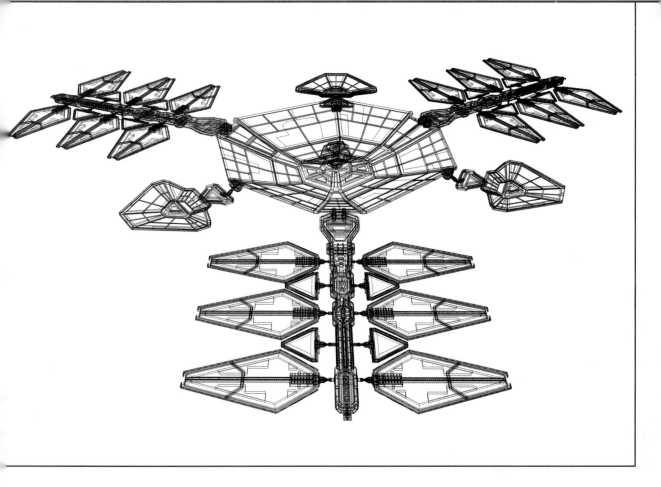

SPECIFICATIONS

Dimensions:
  Overall Length: 293.3 meters
  Overall Beam: 250.6 meters
  Overall Draft: 20 meters (with graviton emitters not active)
Displacement: 133,720 metric tons
Crew Complement: NONE
Velocity: N/A
Acceleration: N/A
Duration:
  Open-Ended; Projected 10 Years Before Major Upgrades

Propulsion Systems:
  8 Particle Beam Thrusters
Weapons: NONE
Primary Computer System: M-16 Bio-Neural Gelpack
  Isolinear III Processor
Primary Navigation System: Stellar Dynamic Position
  Control System
Deflector Systems: FSD Primary Force Field and Deflector
  Control System

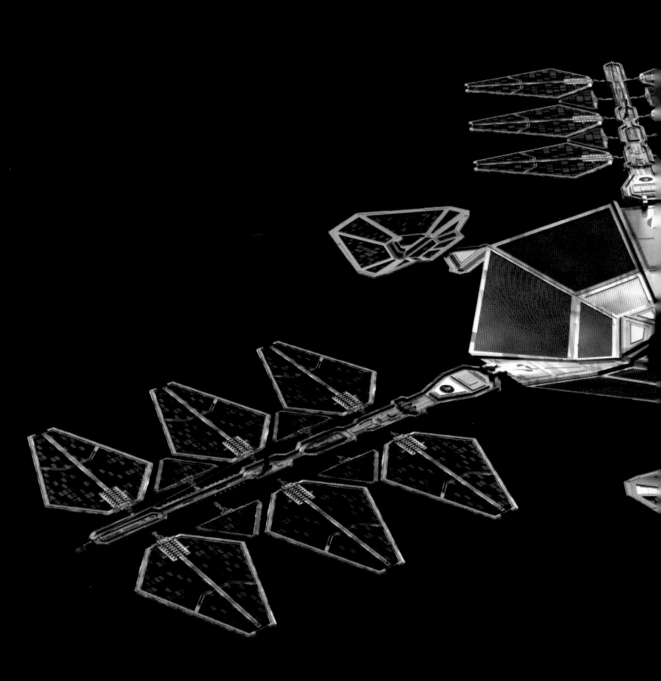

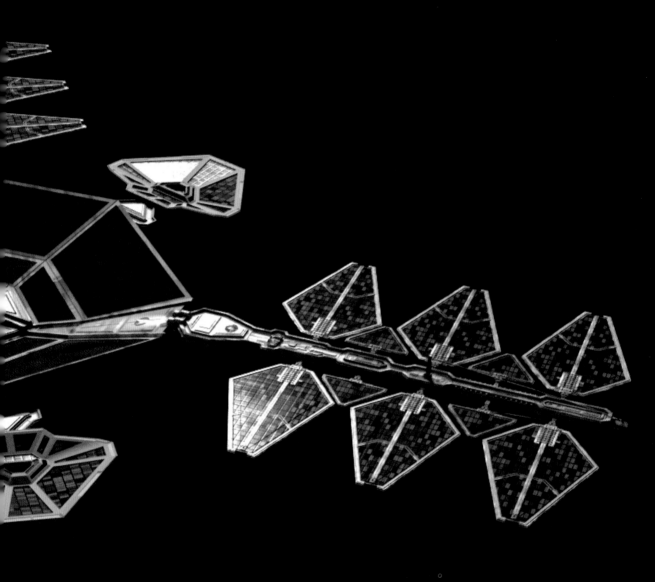

KLINGON HEAVY BATTLE CRUISER

K'T'INGA-CLASS FIRST ENCOUNTERED: 2270

MISSION

During the 2260s, Federation forces found themselves in frequent skirmishes with the Klingons, encountering the all-too-familiar (D-7) battle cruiser. The Klingon Empire began to perceive the Federation as a significant threat to their power. Considerable resources went into redesign and upgrade of the D-7 resulting in the substantially more advanced and powerful *K't'inga*-class heavy battle cruiser. The Klingon intention was to maintain the Empire and minimize the possibility that the Defense Force could be successfully challenged. The *K't'inga*-class would be the instrument of obtaining parity with the Federation, if not achieving outright military superiority.

FEATURES

Although outwardly quite similar to the basic hull design of its predecessor the D-7, the *K't'inga*-class brought forward a number of new and important features in the evolution of the Klingon battle cruiser. The most significant breakthrough was a more thoroughly comparted-mented hull, designed to withstand heavy weapons fire and multiple breaches. Internal areas could be sealed off using either force fields or bulkheads. Like most Klingon vessels, the *K't'inga*-class was designed with no extra comforts for its crew. Even cargo areas could be converted to quarters. Finally, the weapons upgrade on the *K't'inga*-class was quite significant. Unlike the D-7, which used phaserlike weapons batteries in addition to disruptors, the beam weapon of the *K't'inga*-class armament consisted entirely of disruptors operating at enhanced power levels. Added to its impressive beam ordnance array, the *K't'inga*-class also had torpedo tubes mounted both fore and aft, allowing for a wide range of weapons targeting.

The *K't'inga*-class was also notable for being equipped with a cloaking device. In 2268, the Romulan Star Empire entered into an alliance with the Klingon Empire. The Romulans gained access to Klingon vessel designs, and the Klingons were given the specifications for the Romulan cloaking device. Since then, cloaking devices have been standard issue on ships of the Klingon Defense Force.

BACKGROUND

Like the refit *Constitution*-class starship of Starfleet, the *K't'inga*-class heavy battle cruiser was the final evolution of the design built in that general configuration. Unlike the *Constitution*-class refit, the *K't'inga*-class heavy battle cruisers remained in service throughout the next century, receiving ongoing technological upgrades to maintain their capabilities as front-line combat spacecraft. Vessels of this class could be found at many key historical events, including the signing of the Khitomer Accords (2293), the assault on Space Station Deep Space 9 (2372) and they saw extensive service in the Dominion War. No longer in production, the remaining *K't'inga*-class ships are viewed as a living link to the honored warriors of the past. The vessels are treated with respect and extraordinary service is given to them by their crews.

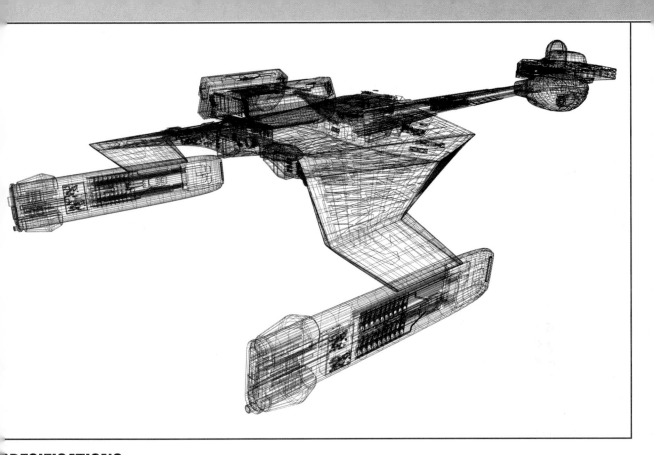

SPECIFICATIONS

Dimensions:
    Overall Length: 214.3 meters
    Overall Beam: 152.4 meters
    Overall Draft: 57.3 meters
Displacement: 120,000 metric tons
Crew Complement: 385 persons
Velocity*:
    Cruising: Warp Factor 6
    Maximum: Warp Factor 10
Acceleration*:
    Rest-Onset Critical Momentum: 4.74 sec
    Onset Critical Momentum-Warp Engage: 1.42 sec
    Warp 1-Warp 4: 0.80 sec
    Warp 4-Warp 6: 0.64 sec
    Warp 6-Warp 10: 2.11 sec

Duration:
    Standard Mission: 8 years
    Recommended Yard Overhaul: 16 years
Propulsion Systems:
    Warp: (2) STN5 Dilithium Conversion Graf Units
    Impulse: (2) Hydrogen Energy Impulse Units
Weapons:
    8 Gravitic Disruptor Mounts
    2 T Yagust Type Photon Torpedo Tubes
Primary Computer System: Ku-Tan Level 15 Central Processor
Primary Navigation System: Druim-Blinge Vector
    and Tensor Analysis System
Deflector Systems: Zigarktar Deflector Plating
    and Field Generation
Embarked Craft (Typical):
    6 General Utility Craft
    8 Shuttlecraft (various classes)

*Velocity and acceleration figures reflect the rated specifications in the Original Cochrane Unit (OCU) warp scale as set prior to 2312, after which time Starfleet adopted the Modified Cochrane Unit (MCU) warp scale.

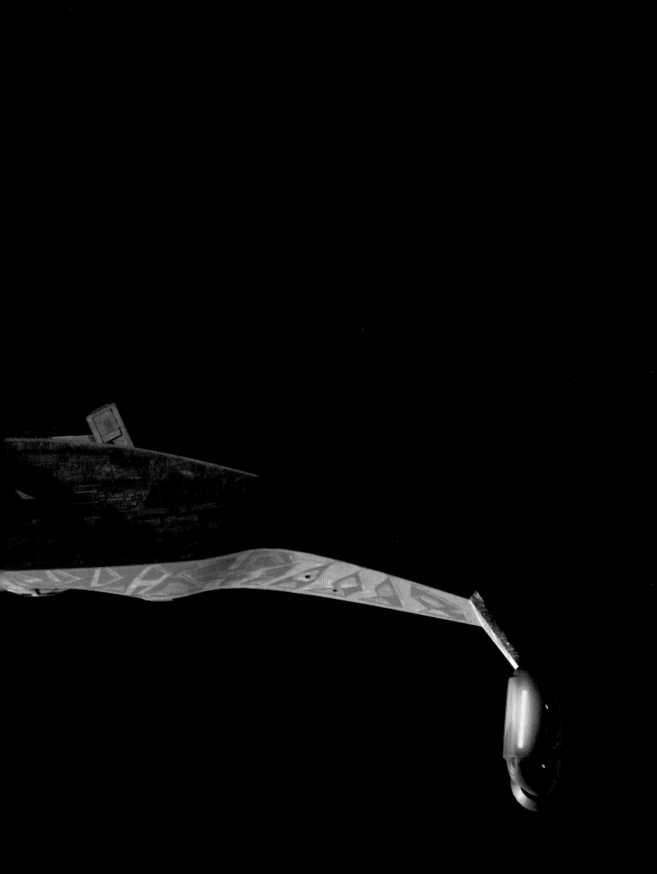

KLINGON BIRD-OF-PREY

B'REL-CLASS FIRST ENCOUNTERED: 2282

MISSION

Despite its small size, the *B'rel*-class posed a significant threat to enemies of the Klingon Empire. A scout ship developed in 2270, the *B'rel*-class fulfilled the Empire's need for a small, fast vessel that could move with stealth through hostile territories and strike quickly and effectively against the Empire's foes.

FEATURES

The *B'rel*-class depended heavily on its cloaking device to allow the ship to carry out its missions. Designed to operate stealthily and quickly, a cloaked bird-of-prey (a term coined by Starfleet) could travel through territory with minimal risk of detection. The only drawback was the ship could not engage weapons systems while cloaked. The ability of the *B'rel*-class to make planetfall was another important feature. This allowed the ship to double as a base of operations for a small expeditionary force. Finally, the *B'rel*-class had adjustable wings that allowed for maximum operating efficiency. The wings could be lowered into an attack position, raised to serve as airfoils for planetary operations, or kept flat for regular cruising, either in space or in an atmosphere.

BACKGROUND

Initially developed from a Romulan concept, the final design of the *B'rel*-class still bears the distinct birdlike markings echoing its Romulan origins. From inception, the *B'rel*-class proved itself an extremely effective addition to the Klingon Defense Force. The *B'rel*-class quickly found itself to be exceedingly popular with commanders and crews. Birds-of-prey became well known for engagements against the *U.S.S. Enterprise* (NCC-1701 and NCC-1701-A), during the Genesis incident, a flight through the Great Barrier at the center of the Milky Way Galaxy, and the battle in the Khitomer system before the signing of the Khitomer Accords.

The solid and effective design of the *B'rel*-class led the Klingons to further develop the class. By the second quarter of the twenty-fourth century, a larger model of this design had been commissioned: the *K'vort*-class cruiser. The *B'rel*-class has continued in service and still plays an important role within the Klingon Defense Force today.

SPECIFICATIONS

Dimensions:
  Overall Length: 88 meters
  Overall Beam: 130 meters
  Overall Draft: 21.7 meters
Displacement: 46,300 metric tons
Crew Complement: 12 persons
Velocity*:
  Cruising: Warp Factor 7
  Maximum: Warp Factor 8
Acceleration*:
  Rest-Onset Critical Momentum: 6.11 sec
  Onset Critical Momentum-Warp Engage: 0.76 sec
  Warp 1-Warp 4: 0.97 sec
  Warp 4-Warp 7: 1.12 sec
  Warp 7-Warp 8: 3.24 sec

Duration:
  Standard Mission: 2 years
  Recommended Yard Overhaul: 10 years
Propulsion Systems:
  Warp: (1) KWC Dilithium Conversion Graf Unit
  Impulse: (1) Hydrogen Energy Integrated Impulse Drive Unit
Weapons:
  2 Gravitic Disruptor Mounts
  1 Type KP-5 Photon Torpedo Tube
Primary Computer System: ZD-4 Level 12 Central Processor
Primary Navigation System: Druim-Blinge Vector and Tensor
  Analysis System
Deflector Systems: Deflector Plating and Field Generation
  System

*Velocity and acceleration figures reflect the rated specifications in the Original Cochrane Unit (OCU) warp scale as set prior to 2312, after which time Starfleet adopted the Modified Cochrane Unit (MCU) warp scale.

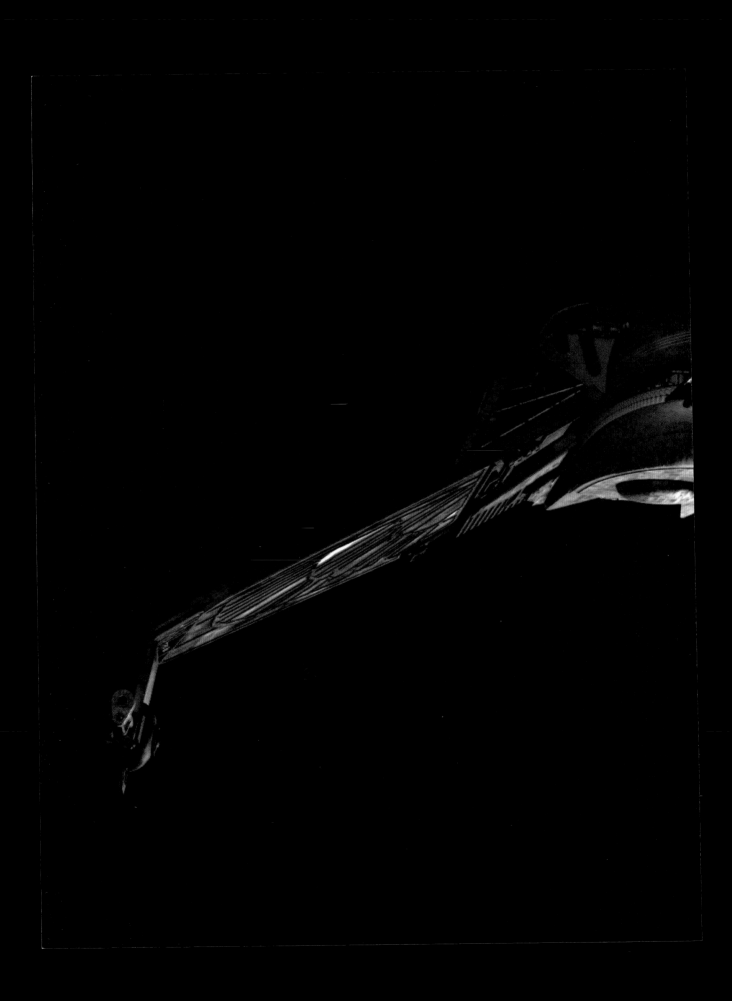

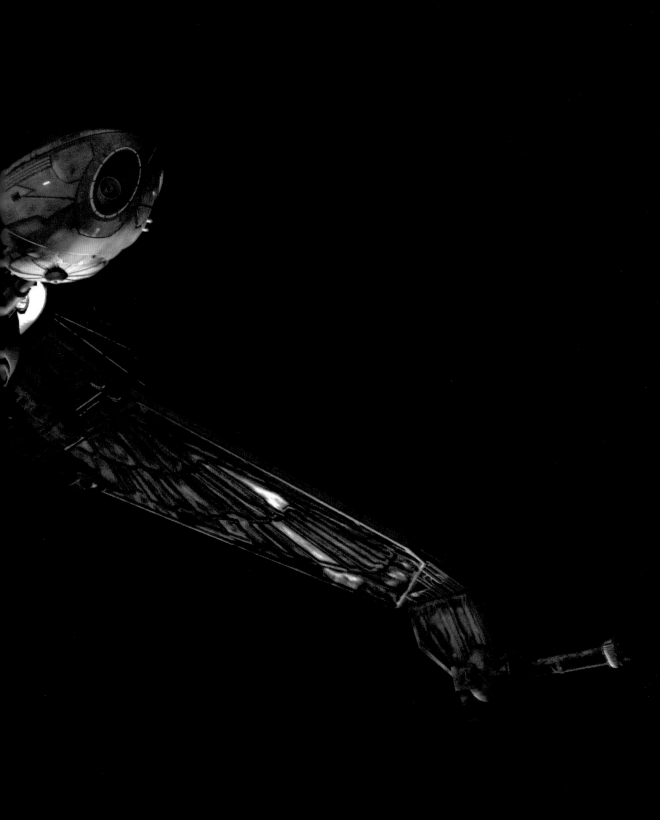

KLINGON ATTACK CRUISER

VOR'CHA-CLASS   FIRST ENCOUNTERED: 2367

MISSION

The primary fighting vessel of the Klingon Defense Force, the *Vor'cha*-class attack cruiser is often seen as the flagship in fleets held by the Great Houses of the Empire. One of the first major applications of new shipbuilding technologies to the Klingon fleet after the *K't'inga*-class of the late twenty-third century, the *Vor'cha*-class carries with it the responsibility of continuing to demonstrate Klingon military strength and readiness. A multimission vessel, the *Vor'cha*-class functions primarily as a combat vessel, and its structure and design are geared for efficient combat capability.

FEATURES

The general design of the *Vor'cha*-class echoes traditional Klingon configurations, with a smaller command hull on the forward end of a long boom, connected to a wide secondary hull with the warp nacelles mounted outboard. The forward command hull contains a powerful disruptor cannon, one of the largest ship-mounted weapons. As is typical for Klingon vessels, the *Vor'cha*-class attack cruiser is equipped with a cloaking device for stealth mode travel. Some aspects of the *Vor'cha*-class design reflect Starfleet technologies exchanged during the years of détente. The Starfleet influence can be seen in the Bussard collectors mounted on the forward ends of the nacelles. However, these collectors are supplemental to the ram intakes on the wings.

BACKGROUND

Klingons do not typically design new classes of warship entirely from scratch. By the early twenty-fourth century, the Empire discovered that the long-used D-7 battle cruisers were quickly becoming outmoded, as both Starfleet and the Romulans developed larger and more powerful ships. The Klingon Empire decided to develop a new and much more powerful cruiser. This *Vor'cha*-class quickly brought the Klingons back up to parity with both the United Federation of Planets and the Romulan Star Empire.

While the recently developed, larger *Negh'Var*-class vessel is more powerful, the *Vor'cha*-class continues as the most utilized starship throughout the Klingon Empire. The *Vor'cha*-class remains the easiest and fastest ship to deploy to trouble-spots. Utilized successfully throughout countless combat offensives during the Dominion War, the *Vor'cha*-class has proudly and honorably served as a primary instrument in the Klingon Defense Force.

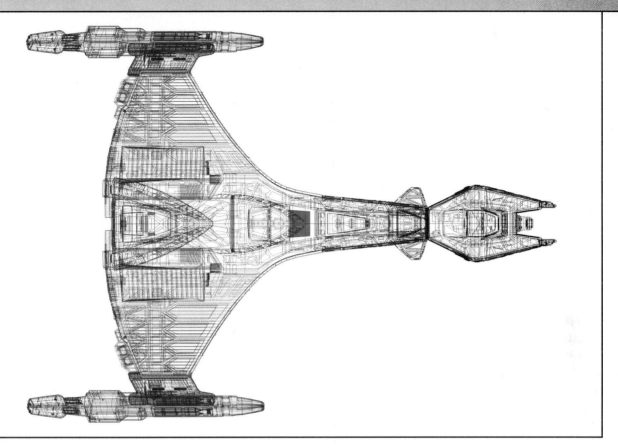

SPECIFICATIONS

Dimensions:
  Overall Length: 481.3 meters
  Overall Beam: 341.8 meters
  Overall Draft: 106.9 meters
Displacement: 2,238,000 metric tons
Crew Complement: 1,900 persons
Velocity:
  Cruising: Warp Factor 6
  Maximum: Warp Factor 9.6
Acceleration:
  Rest-Onset Critical Momentum: 5.85 sec
  Onset Critical Momentum-Warp Engage: 1.48 sec
  Warp 1-Warp 4: 1.02 sec
  Warp 4-Warp 6: 075 sec
  Warp 6-Warp 9.6: 3.43 sec
Duration:
  Standard Mission: 2 years
  Recommended Yard Overhaul: 6 years

Propulsion Systems:
  Warp: (2) STN8A Dilithium Conversion Graf Units
  Impulse: (2) Hydrogen Energy Impulse Units
Weapons:
  18 Gravitic Disruptor Mounts
  3 'etlh'a' Type Photon Torpedo Tubes
Primary Computer System: Ku-Tan Level 20 Central Processor
Primary Navigation System: Advanced *Hov' buS* Vector and
  Tensor Analysis System
Deflector Systems:
  16 Deflector Plating and Field Generation System
Embarked Craft (Typical):
  12 General Utility Craft
  25 Shuttlecraft (various classes)

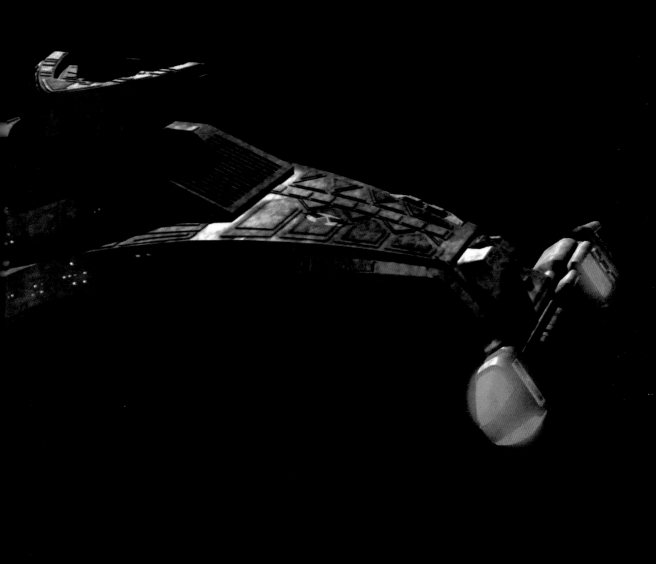

BIRD-OF-PREY

ROMULAN SPACECRAFT   FIRST ENCOUNTERED: 2266

MISSION

Relatively little is known about this early Romulan warship. When first encountered by the Federation in the mid twenty-third century, the bird-of-prey cruiser was believed to be the mainstay of the Romulan fleet. Small and compact, this cruiser featured few comforts and was primarily designed to display and project force for the furtherance of the Empire's goals. In its early encounters with the Federation, this vessel was seen testing Starfleet's defenses along the Romulan Neutral Zone, apparently attempting to determine how the Federation might respond.

FEATURES

The bird-of-prey was most notable for two key systems: its focused energy plasma weapon and the surprising introduction of the never-before-encountered cloaking device. The plasma weapon itself took up a substantial portion of the interior of the ship, but was devastatingly effective at short and medium ranges. Unfortunately for the Romulans, while powerful, the plasma bolts were limited in range and dissipated to a weakened intensity the more distance they covered. Encounters with this vessel by the *Starship Enterprise* (2266) allowed Starfleet to develop tactics to circumvent the weapon. The cloaking device was a significantly more challenging element. Countermeasures developed by the Federation spurred the Romulans to improve the cloak, and that would lead to improved Starfleet sensors. This ever escalating cycle, many in the Intelligence community believe, led the Romulans to share the cloak technology with the Klingons. While short lived, the alliance led to the end of the bird-of-prey production. This escalation would continue until the Treaty of Algeron.

BACKGROUND

The year was 2266, the Federation and the Romulans Star Empire had not encountered each other in over a century. A series of mysterious attacks on Federation outposts along the Romulan Neutral Zone resulted in Starfleet dispatching the *U.S.S. Enterprise* NCC-1701 to investigate. The *Enterprise* encountered a single bird-of-prey. While significantly smaller, it nearly destroyed the starship. Fortunately, the tactics of the *Enterprise* crew allowed the starship to emerge victorious.

True to the Romulan strategy of testing an enemy first to determine the most effective means to achieve victory, the loss of this single bird-of-prey alerted the Empire that Starfleet had also progressed substantially. The Romulans quickly initiated an ambitious fleet upgrade program. Seeing the Federation as a more significant threat than the Romulans, the Klingon Empire initially provided the Romulans with D-7 battle cruisers. The last of this class of bird-of-prey was removed from service early in the twenty-fourth century.

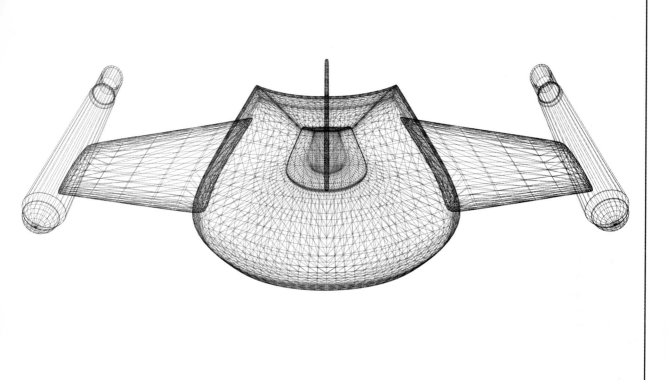

SPECIFICATIONS

Dimensions:
    Overall Length: 68.2 meters
    Overall Beam: 90.6 meters
    Overall Draft: 21.9 meters
Displacement: 25,000 metric tons
Crew Complement: 170 persons
Velocity*:
    Cruising: Warp Factor 6
    Maximum: Warp Factor 8
Acceleration*:
    Rest-Onset Critical Momentum: 5.62 sec
    Onset Critical Momentum-Warp Engage: 1.11 sec
    Warp 1-Warp 4: 6.68 sec
    Warp 4-Warp 6: 2.14 sec
    Warp 6-Warp 8: 4.09 sec

Duration:
    Standard Mission: 2 years
    Recommended Yard Overhaul: 8 years
Propulsion Systems:
    Warp: (2) RWC-1 Warp Drive Units
    Impulse: (6) RIB-1 Nuclear Fusion Impulse Units
Weapons:
    1 RPL-2 Focused Energy Plasma Weapon
    10 Direct-Fire Nuclear Fusion Missile Tubes
Primary Computer System: R4M Advanced
    Cybernetic Processor
Primary Navigation System: UNKNOWN
Deflector Systems: UNKNOWN
Embarked Craft (Typical):
    2 Shuttlecraft (3-person small shuttles)

*Velocity and acceleration figures reflect the rated specifications in the Original Cochrane Unit (OCU) warp scale as set prior to 2312, after which time Starfleet adopted the Modified Cochrane Unit (MCU) warp scale.

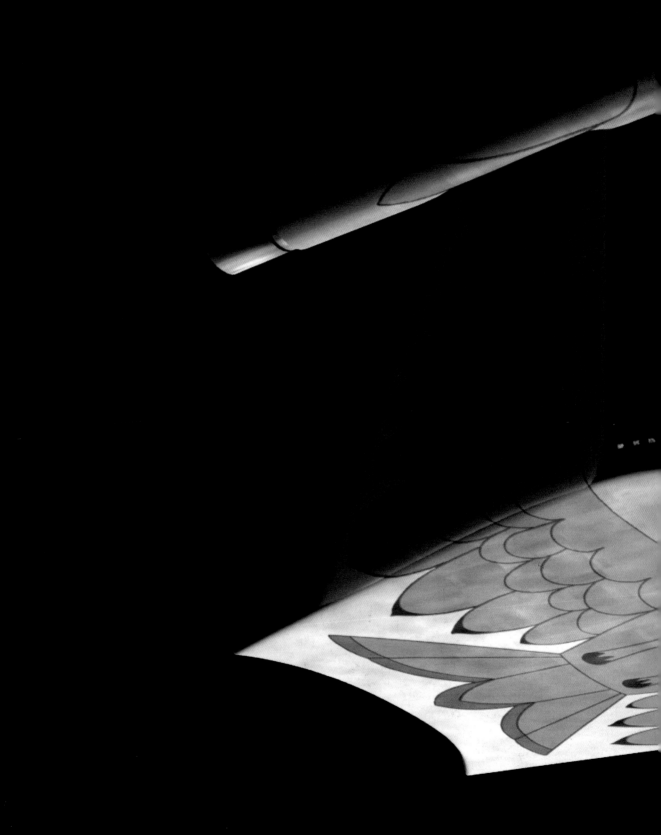

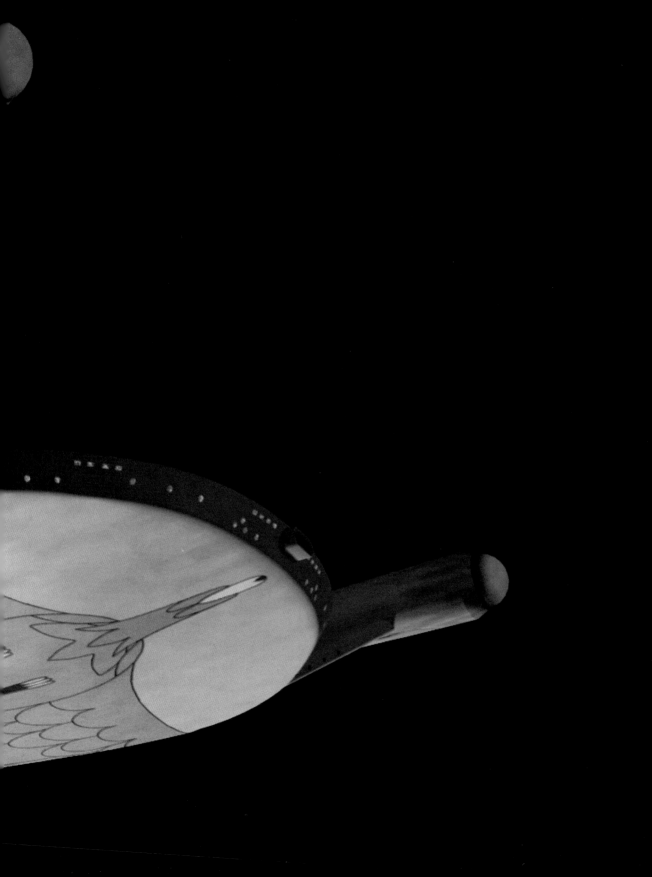

ROMULAN WARBIRD

D'DERIDEX-CLASS   FIRST ENCOUNTERED: 2349

MISSION

The *D'deridex*-class warbird is the core of the Romulan Imperial Fleet. One of the largest vessels in known space, the warbird design intentionally projects an image of power and menace. Multimission vehicles, the warbirds serve most effectively in combat, threat engagement and containment situations. The sheer power and size of the *D'deridex*-class is often enough to daunt opponents. The vessels have large cargo spaces for materiel, apparatus, and supplies for other ships, bases, and colonies.

FEATURES

The Romulan fleet is visually distinctive, the hulls of Romulan vessels are a bright green color. Another unusual feature of the *D'deridex*-class is its dual hull configuration, with the aft section divided into separate upper and lower segments. Most Romulan vessels have adopted a power-source that is unusual: an artificial quantum singularity. This power source serves the same purpose as the matter/antimatter reactors used by other warp capable life-forms. As with other Romulan vessels, the warbird carries an advanced cloaking device. Certain radiations or core emissions can compromise the cloak, so these elements must be monitored carefully. As a result, the warbird limits subspace transmissions while under cloak.

BACKGROUND

First constructed in the middle of the twenty-fourth century, the *D'deridex*-class warbird is a direct descendent of the warbird designs of the late twenty-third century. The *D'deridex*-class refined and improved upon the most critical design elements of those ships, greatly advancing the military capabilities and power of the Romulan Star Empire. Those refinements, along with a proven maneuverability against other vessels, made the warbird the most effective vessel of the Romulan fleet, a position it had held for the last three decades.

Vessels of the *D'deridex*-class have been involved in a number of significant actions, including the first official contact made with Starfleet since the Tomed Incident. Once contact had been made in 2364, with the *Starship Enterprise*, warbirds were commonly seen in neutral areas of space. There were also a few "muscle-flexing" encounters where warbirds locked disruptors on ships of Starfleet and the Klingon Defense Forces.

The *D'deridex*-class served with great distinction throughout the Dominion War. They were an essential part of the forces at the Battle of Chin'toka, and the final assault on Cardassia Prime. Refits began to the *D'deridex*-class ships in 2378 and are projected to be completed within the next three years. It is expected that these refits and system upgrades will ensure the *D'deridex*-class warbird remains in service into the twenty-fifth century.

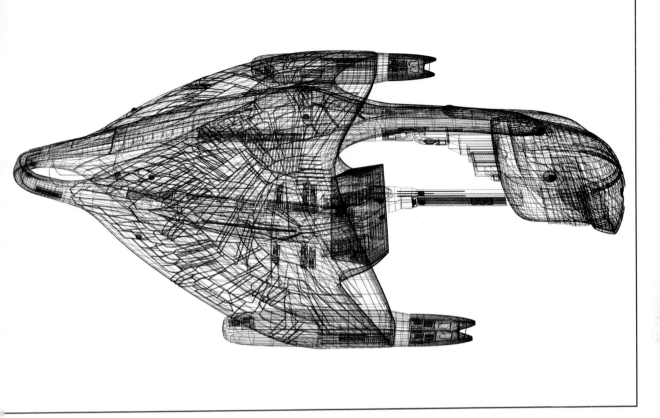

SPECIFICATIONS

Dimensions:
  Overall Length: 1,041.7 meters
  Overall Beam: 772.4 meters
  Overall Draft: 285.5 meters
Displacement: 4,320,000 metric tons
Crew Complement: 1,500 persons
Velocity:
  Cruising: Warp Factor 5
  Maximum: Warp Factor 9.6
Acceleration:
  Rest-Onset Critical Momentum: 6.98 sec
  Onset Critical Momentum-Warp Engage: 2.34 sec
  Warp 1-Warp 3: 4.72 sec
  Warp 3-Warp 5: 3.56 sec
  Warp 5-Warp 9.6: 5.44 sec
Duration:
  Standard Mission: 4 years
  Recommended Yard Overhaul: 17 years

Propulsion Systems:
  Warp: (2) Type 5C6 Quantum Singularity Energized
    Warp Drive Units
  Impulse: (2) Class 4A Augmented Nuclear Fusion
    Impulse Units
Weapons:
  6 Primary-Focus Disruptor Arrays
  2 Direct-Fire Photon Torpedo Tubes
Primary Computer System: UNKNOWN
Primary Navigation System: UNKNOWN
Deflector Systems: UNKNOWN
Embarked Craft (Typical):
  16 Shuttlecraft (various classes)
  8 Shuttlepods (various classes)

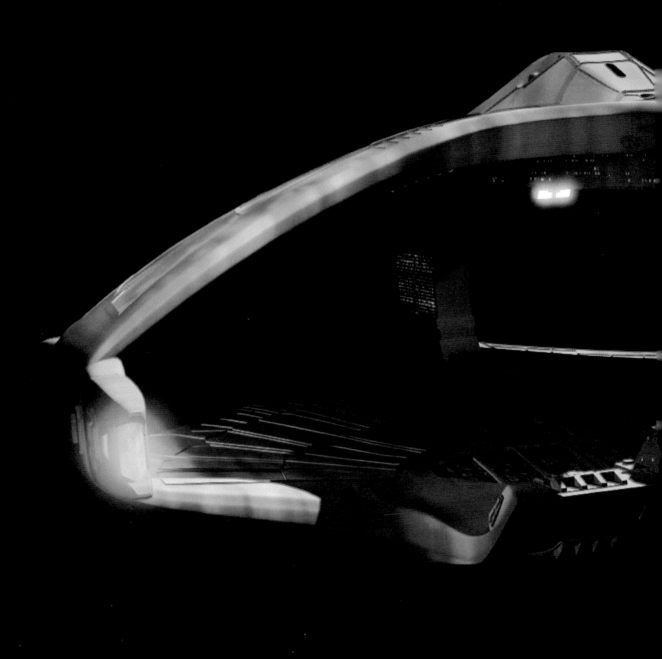

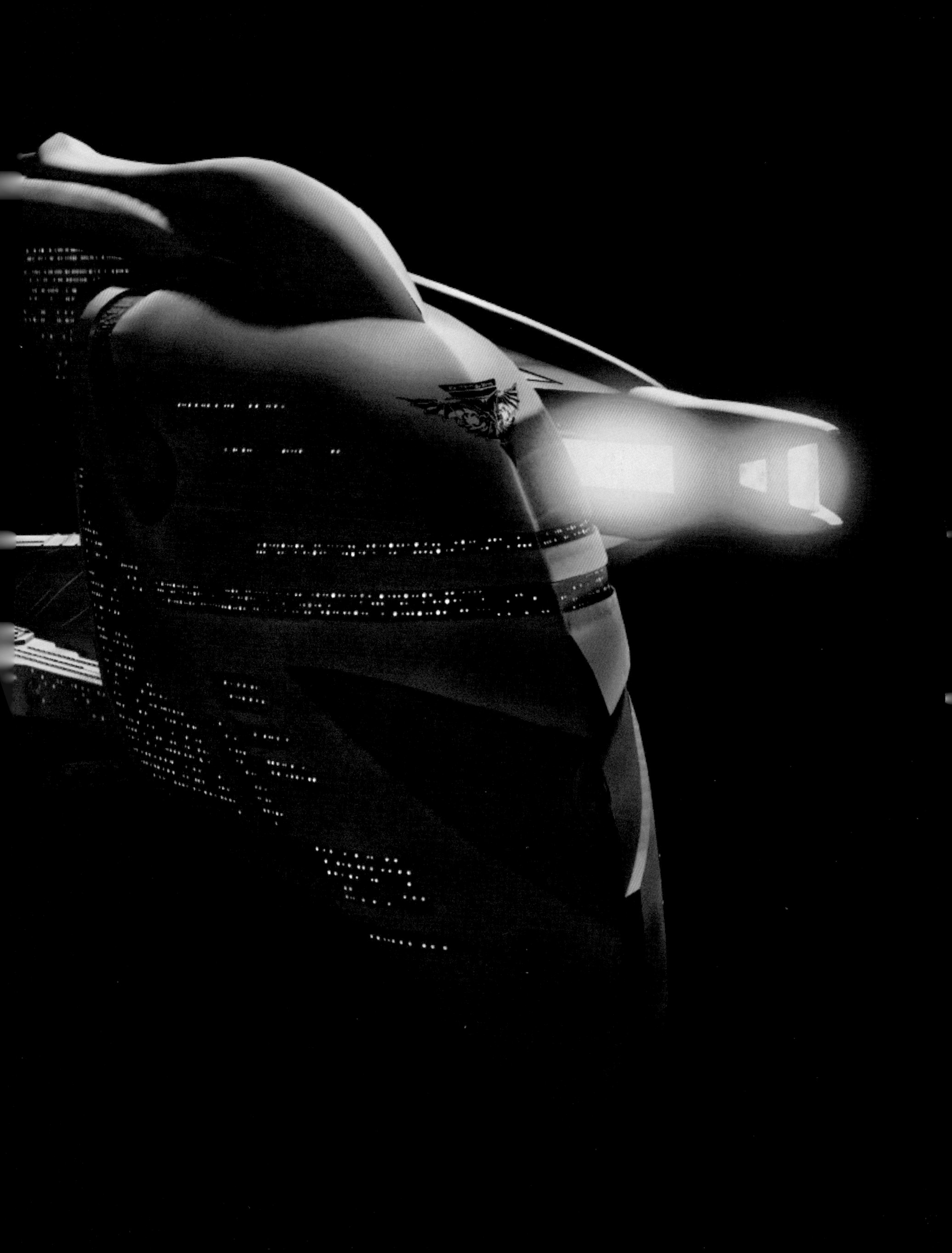

CARDASSIAN WARSHIP

GALOR-CLASS   FIRST ENCOUNTERED: 2355

MISSION

The primary combat and defense vessel of the Cardassian Union is the *Galor*-class spacecraft. The primary role this ship played has bee as an instrument of Cardassian military policy. While not perceived as a particularly effective research vessel by Federation observers, th *Galor*-class combat performance is extremely impressive, particularly for a ship of its size. The *Galor*-class has also been utilized as a troo transport vessel, an escort ship, an orbital assault platform, and a blockade vessel.

FEATURES

A smaller ship relative to many of the other vessels of the Alpha and Beta Quadrant powers, the *Galor*-class is highly effective. Like othe Cardassian vessels, the *Galor*-class is recognizable for its unusual warp nacelle configuration. The nacelles are mounted in the wings at th forward section of the ship. Also unusual is the design of the spiral-wave disruptors. This unique and effective weapons system has posed sig nificant tactical challenges for many vessels engaging a *Galor*-class spacecraft.

BACKGROUND

The *Galor*-class spacecraft was first encountered by Starfleet forces during the Cardassian conflicts of the 2350s. At the time, Cardassian and Starfleet forces appeared to be evenly matched. Typical Cardassian strategy involved gaining an early advantage and exploiting that posi tion to gain victory by overwhelming an opponent. Another advantage the Cardassians had was Starfleet's lack of knowledge abou Cardassian military technology. Cardassian vessels have dampening fields and special shielding which were developed to block sensor scans Many ship commanders unilaterally decided that if their vessels were damaged in battle beyond the ability to retreat, they ordered the destruction of their vessels.

The Cardassian Union eventually ceased hostilities with Starfleet and withdrew. Contact with the Federation was kept to a minimum fo more than a decade while the Cardassian Union rebuilt and augmented its fleet. Any attempt by Starfleet to learn more about ship desigr was foiled by the considerable prowess of the Obsidian Order.

By the Dominion War, Starfleet still knew very little about Cardassian military capabilities. When the Cardassian Union allied itself with the Dominion against the Federation and the Klingon Empire, the results were devastating for the forces of Starfleet.

Now enjoying a more peaceful and direct contact with the Cardassian Union, the Federation has begun to learn much more about Cardassian spacecraft. Among the first pieces of information exchanged was the meaning of the class name *Galor*. While not a strategically valuable piece of intelligence, this open offering of information was symbolic of a new era of friendship between the two former enemies. *Galor* was a hooded warrior from Cardassian mythology. *Galor* commanded great respect among his people for his victories in battle.

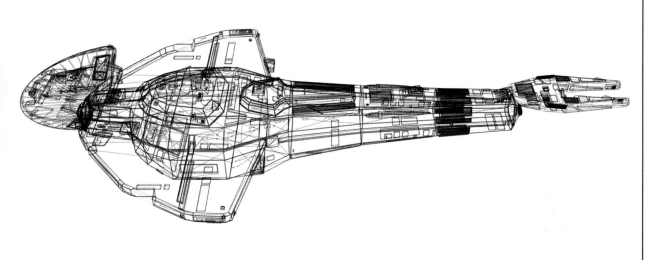

SPECIFICATIONS

Dimensions:
    Overall Length: 229.5 meters
    Overall Beam: 118.7 meters
    Overall Draft: 38.1 meters
Displacement: 412,930 metric tons
Crew Complement: 300 persons
Velocity:
    Cruising: Warp Factor 5
    Maximum: Warp Factor 9.6
Acceleration:
    Rest-Onset Critical Momentum: 5.85 sec
    Onset Critical Momentum-Warp Engage: 2.01 sec
    Warp 1-Warp 4: 1.80 sec
    Warp 4-Warp 5: 0.52 sec
    Warp 5-Warp 9.6: 5.26 sec

Duration:
    Standard Mission: 3 years.
    Recommended Yard Overhaul: 7 years
Propulsion Systems:
    Warp: (2) Type 5 DC Warp Drive Units
    Impulse: (3) Hydrogen Energy Impulse Units
Weapons (Known):
    8 Spiral Wave Disruptor Mounts
    1 Aft-Mount Disruptor-Wave Cannon
Primary Computer System: CLASSIFIED
Primary Navigation System: CLASSIFIED
Deflector Systems: UNKNOWN
Embarked Craft (Typical):
    15 Fighters and Shuttlecraft (various classes)

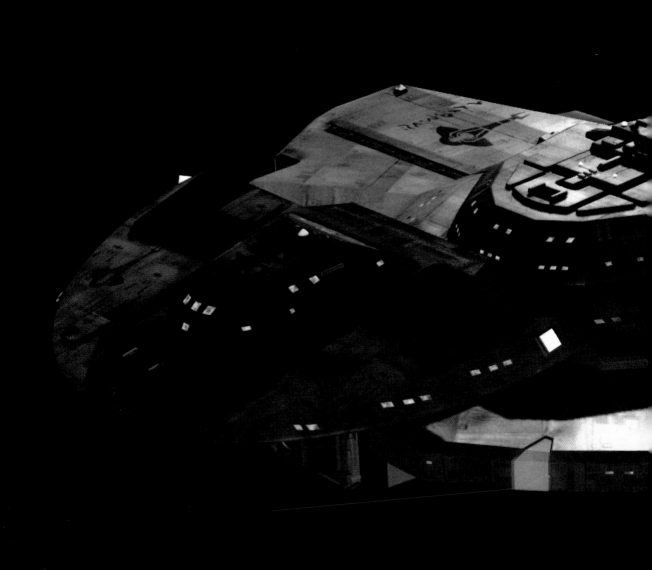

JEM'HADAR ATTACK SHIP

FIRST ENCOUNTERED: 2370

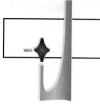

MISSION

The Jem'Hadar attack ship is a direct, straightforward vessel directed toward a single purpose: to defeat any force posing a threat to the Dominion. These deadly ships have been utilized extensively by the Dominion throughout the Gamma Quadrant and have threatened the Federation and its allies during the recent Dominion War. The attack ship carries a Jem'Hadar crew who are focused solely on the defeat of the enemy. All elements of the vessel's design exist to support this one purpose.

FEATURES

Fast and maneuverable, the Jem'Hadar attack ship serves effectively as a hard-hitting weapon and instrument of war. Its phased polaron beam weapons can cripple much larger enemy vessels, and its deflectors are designed to repel not only incoming weapons fire, but also tractor beams. Main power derives from a highly efficient matter/antimatter reactor. In addition to the standard warp and impulse engine systems, the attack ship employs an ion drive as a secondary propulsion system. Jem'Hadar attack ships typically operate in groups of three, using maneuverability and combined firepower to overwhelm an enemy vessel's defenses through a continuous weapons barrage.

BACKGROUND

Jem'Hadar attack ships have proven themselves as vexing opponents. For several years after Starfleet's first encounters with this small yet powerful ship, the Corp of Engineers were stymied in figuring out how to deal effectively with this threat. In 2373, a Starfleet science team discovered a crashed Jem'Hadar attack ship on Torga IV in the Gamma Quadrant. After a brief standoff with the surviving crew, Starfleet personnel captured the craft. Starfleet was able to study it in detail and began developing counterattack strategies. Among the few weaknesses Starfleet scientists discovered was a vulnerability to attacks from directly above because of shield weaknesses at the dorsal field junctions along the upper hull.

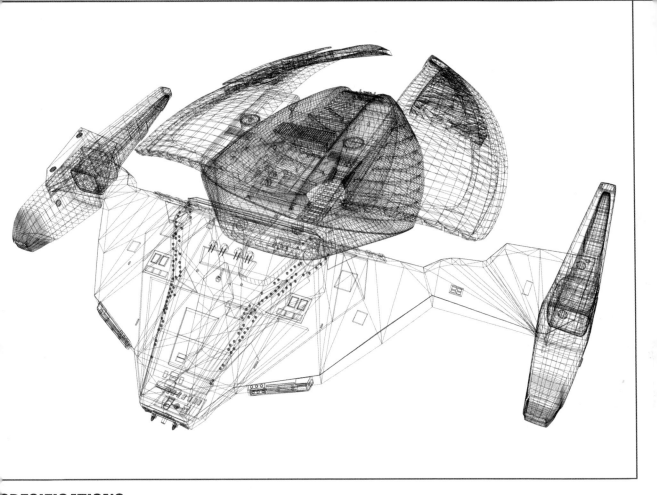

SPECIFICATIONS

Dimensions:
   Overall Length: 68.3 meters
   Overall Beam: 70.02 meters
   Overall Draft: 18.3 meters
Displacement: 2,450 metric tons
Crew Complement: 16
Velocity:
   Cruising: Warp Factor 5
   Maximum: Warp Factor 9.6
Acceleration:
   Rest-Onset Critical Momentum: 6.11 sec (est.)
   Onset Critical Momentum-Warp Engage: 2.06 sec (est.)
   Warp 1-Warp 4: 0.92 sec
   Warp 4-Warp 6: 0.81 sec
   Warp 6-Warp 9.6: 3.25 sec

Duration:
   Standard Mission: UNKNOWN
   Recommended Yard Overhaul: UNKNOWN
Propulsion Systems:
   Warp: (2) Ion Propulsion Units
   Impulse: (1) Ventral Impellers Impulse Unit
Weapons:
   4 Polaron Beam Emitters
Primary Computer System: CLASSIFIED
Primary Navigation System: CLASSIFIED
Deflector Systems: CLASSIFIED
Embarked Craft (Typical): CLASSIFIED

MALON EXPORT VESSEL

DELTA QUADRANT WASTE DISPOSAL FREIGHTER   FIRST ENCOUNTERED: 2375

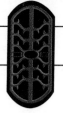

MISSION

The Malon used matter-antimatter reactions as an energy source for their society. They had not, as of 2375, developed the technology to purify the contaminated antimatter. As such, the Malon produced over six billion isotons of contaminated antimatter each day, giving off lethal doses of deadly theta radiation. It is not surprising that waste disposal of these large amounts of contaminated antimatter became a business endeavor on Malon Prime. A fleet of export vessels of varying sizes were employed for the single purpose of disposing of—more precisely, dumping—this waste in areas of space far from Malon Prime. Little more than garbage scows, these vessels fulfilled a significant role in the economy and day-to-day operation of Malon society.

FEATURES

The vast majority of the Malon export vessel was committed to cargo holds capable of containing over ninety million isotons of contaminated antimatter. Due to the harmful theta radiation emitted by their cargo, Malon export vessels were heavily shielded. The extra shielding also served an important tactical role by making the freighter impervious to many conventional weapons. Concurrently, the Malon had heavily armed their export vessels with multiple spatial charge launchers. This combination of significant armament and shielding was necessary because the Malon had been known to dump their toxic waste in areas of space inhabited by other life-forms, most of whom did not appreciate being the recipients of discarded contaminants.

The export vessels were no cleaner than the waste they transported. Because of their use of unpurified matter-antimatter reactions in their propulsion systems, Malon engines built up critical amounts of reactive by-products as they traversed space. It was not unusual to see Malon export vessels vent explosive bursts of contaminated antimatter, gas, and debris from multiple ports along their hulls.

Several different sizes of freighter were utilized by the Malon to transport their waste products. The vessel pictured here was known as an eleventh gradient class. Larger classes could transport as much as four trillion isotons of contaminated antimatter with a crew of nearly one hundred.

BACKGROUND

You might assume that the Malon would welcome an open offer of technology that could eliminate their waste problem. Yet the Malon were reluctant to accept any form of assistance offered by Captain Kathryn Janeway of the *U.S.S. Voyager*. Concerned about the disastrous effects Malon dumping created throughout a large area of space, Janeway offered to share Federation technology which could purify matter-antimatter reactions and eliminate the need for export vessels. However, with so much of the Malon economic structure dependent upon these export vessels, the offer was refused.

The *Starship Voyager* had three significant encounters with the Malon. During the first, in order to save an innocent race of aliens, Janeway was forced to destroy a Malon export vessel and the spatial vortex it was using to transport waste into that inhabited area of space. During the second encounter, a Malon freighter was destroyed trying to commandeer a *Voyager* probe, and another Malon export vessel later attacked *Voyager* while trying to salvage the same probe. Finally, *Voyager* managed to save an entire sector of space when a Malon freighter carrying a load of over four trillion isotons of contaminated antimatter experienced multiple ruptures in its cargo tanks. By risking *Voyager* and her crew to steer the damaged freighter into an O-type star, where the explosion of deadly theta radiation could be absorbed harmlessly, Janeway protected an area of space encompassing a radius of three light-years.

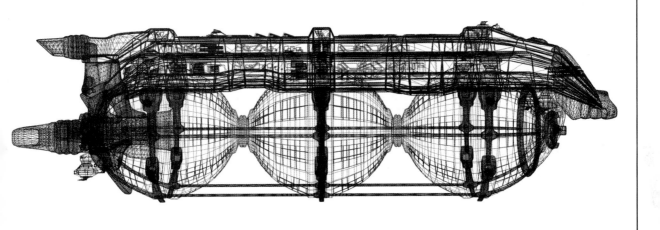

SPECIFICATIONS (FOR 11TH GRADIENT-CLASS FREIGHTER)

Dimensions:
Overall Length: 317.3 meters
Overall Beam: 105.8 meters
Overall Draft: 92.6 meters
Displacement: 1,165,000 metric tons
Crew Complement: 9
Velocity:
Cruising: UNKNOWN
Maximum: UNKNOWN
Acceleration: UNKNOWN
Duration:
Standard Mission: UNKNOWN
Recommended Yard Overhaul: UNKNOWN

Propulsion Systems:
Warp: (3) Unpurified Matter-Antimatter Reactors
(TYPE UNKNOWN)
Impulse: (1) Hydrogen Energy Unit (TYPE UNKNOWN)
Weapons:
12 Spatial Charge Launchers (TYPE UNKNOWN)
Primary Computer System: UNKNOWN
Primary Navigation System: UNKNOWN
Deflector Systems: Reinforced Covariant Shielding and
Tetraburnium Plating
Embarked Craft (Typical): UNKNOWN

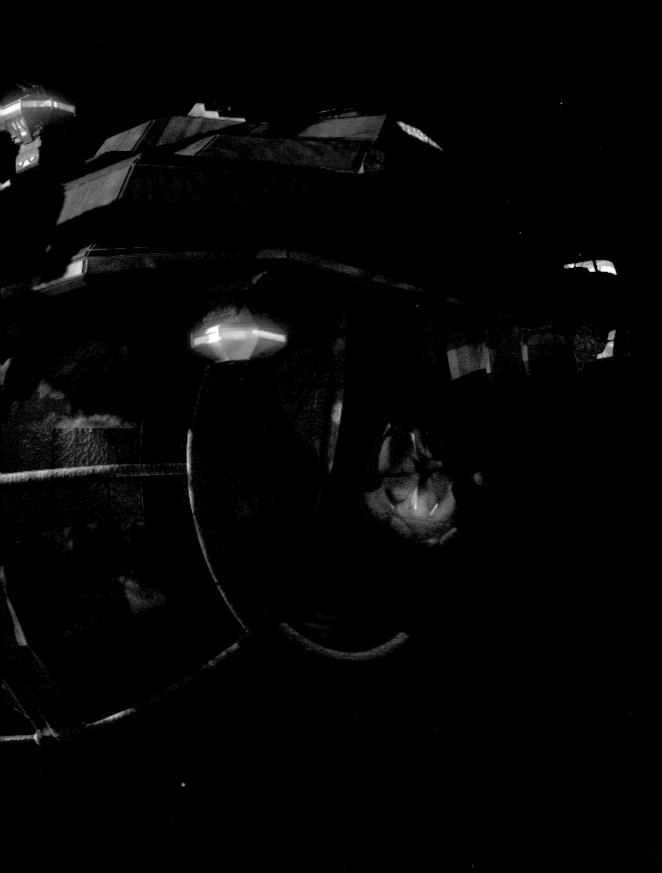

HIROGEN HUNTER VESSEL

DELTA QUADRANT SPACECRAFT   FIRST ENCOUNTERED: 2374

MISSION

With a design completely optimized for the search, acquisition, targeting, pursuit, and capture of prey of all types, the Hirogen hunter vessel is a dreaded sight throughout the Delta Quadrant. A relatively small vehicle, the hunter ship is fast, heavily armed and armored, and highly shielded. With small crews, the hunter ships travel great distances and have succeeded in raiding and effecting the capture of various spacefaring prey. As an instrument of the fundamental Hirogen need to hunt, this vessel is extremely effective.

FEATURES

The hunter vessel's small size belies a number of critical elements that allow it to perform at the level of larger vessels. With a design based entirely on efficiency in tracking and pursuing prey; no extraneous equipment is included. Technology is simply mounted to the exterior of the ship, rather than having it integrated with the ship's structure. Heavily armed for their size, Hirogen vessels carry multiple beam weapon turrets and torpedo launchers. Powerful defensive shielding and monotanium armor plating protect the ship, as the Hirogen have learned that some prey fight back. Powerful warp and sublight impeller drives serve the hunter vessel well, and a "stealth mode" exists to mask engine emissions when the crew wish to track a target vessel without alerting it to their presence.

BACKGROUND

The current Hirogen hunter vessel is heir to a tradition stretching back more than ten thousand years. The location of the Hirogen home world has been lost to the mists of history. As such, Hirogen spacecraft are extremely important to them, and a well-designed hunter ship is critical. The great range of distance that the hunter vessels can traverse is also an intrinsic part of the nomadic nature of the Hirogen. The discovery and takeover of an ancient communications network further expanded their range by allowing greater contact between ships across the vastness of space.

The dispersion of the Hirogen has had a negative side effect, a drop in the population. An encounter with the *U.S.S. Voyager* in 2374 offered a potential solution. In an effort to curb their wide-ranging hunting, Captain Janeway offered to an Alpha Hirogen of one group information on creating holodeck technology. This would allow them to undertake hunts holographically in simulated environments, and not require actual hunts across many light-years. Unfortunately, extensive upgrades of the holotechnology resulted in the Hirogen inadvertently creating a "race" of intelligent holograms with the ability to learn and adapt. The holograms decided to destroy their Hirogen persecutors. *Voyager* stepped in and managed to temporarily end the hostilities. It is not known at this time what ultimately became of the Hirogen or the holotechnology given to them. Follow-up contact with the Hirogen are among the plans for future missions to the Delta Quadrant.

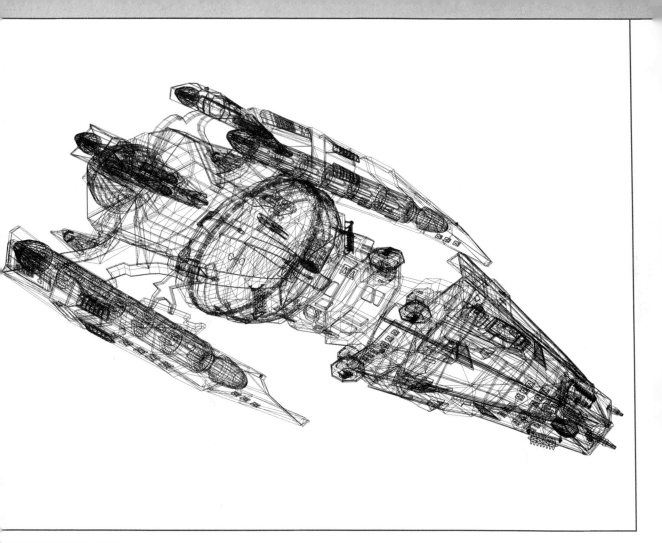

SPECIFICATIONS

Dimensions
  Overall Length: 150 meters
  Overall Beam: 88.9 meters
  Overall Draft: 39.3 meters
Displacement: 56,900 metric tons
Crew Complement: 2-7 persons
Velocity:
  Cruising: UNKNOWN
  Maximum: Warp Factor 8
  Acceleration: UNKNOWN
Duration:
  Standard Mission: UNKNOWN
  Recommended Yard Overhaul: UNKNOWN

Propulsion Systems:
  Warp: (2) Primary Warp Units (TYPE UNKNOWN)
        (2) Secondary Warp Units (TYPE UNKNOWN)
  Impulse: (1) Primary Sublight Impeller Unit (TYPE UNKNOWN)
        (2) Secondary Sublight Impeller Units (TYPE
        UNKNOWN)
Weapons:
  6 Weapons Arrays (TYPE UNKNOWN)
  2 Torpedo Tubes (TYPE (UNKNOWN)
Primary Computer System: UNKNOWN
Primary Navigation System: UNKNOWN
Deflector Systems: UNKNOWN
Embarked Craft (Typical): UNKNOWN

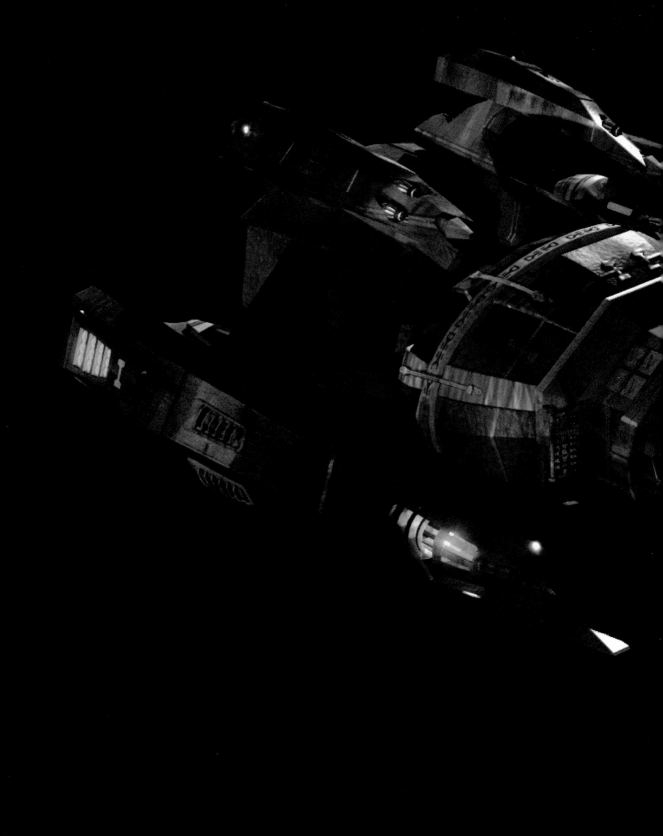

SPECIES 8472 BIOSHIP

ALIEN SPACE VESSEL   FIRST ENCOUNTERED: 2374

MISSION

After only three encounters with Species 8472, each by the *U.S.S. Voyager* while in the Delta Quadrant, the motivations and intentions of this unique alien race remain a mystery to Starfleet Command. Reported to be paranoid, hostile, inquisitive, apprehensive, imperialistic, or simply wishing to be left alone—all are possible profiles for Species 8472. Nothing is known with certainty about the primary mission of the Species 8472 bioship. Heavily armed, it's likely offensive in nature. However, a reconnaissance or scouting role, or even a possible application for scientific exploration cannot be completely ruled out. As with most aspects of Species 8472, Starfleet simply does not wish to speculate.

FEATURES

Organic space vessels are not completely unknown to the Federation: The shapeshifting spaceborne life-form captured by the Bandi people of Deneb IV that took the shape of the Farpoint Station and Gomtuu—known as "Tin Man"—are some examples of living spacecraft. Nevertheless, the Species 8472 bioship is like nothing Starfleet has ever encountered.

Made of the same genetic material as the members of Species 8472, the bioship appears to be piloted by a single individual. Extremely powerful, a single small bioship can easily destroy a Borg cube. Acting as a unit, a group of eight bioships can focus their energy in a ring through a ninth bioship to produce a beam powerful enough to destroy a planet. The bioships appear to be impervious to conventional weapons: phasers, photon torpedoes, and advanced Borg weaponry. The organic material of the bioship is able to quickly heal itself after an attack.

The bioships appear to be powered by antimatter particles and can travel at high warp speeds while also being highly maneuverable. Even more impressive is the ability of even a single bioship to open a quantum singularity as a conduit between our galaxy and the parallel dimension of fluidic space, where Species 8472 originates. The ability to easily traverse such a dimensional rift without being adversely affected by the gravimetric distortions of a singularity suggests that Species 8472 could travel instantaneously to any point in our galaxy.

The surfaces of Species 8472 bioships reflect all deep sensor scans and any true transporter lock. *Voyager* crew members were able to enter one vessel. The inside of the craft contained a chamber forty meters wide with pulsing "veins" functioning as conduits for transporting electrodynamic fluid. The bioship's computer systems also appear to be organic and use neuropeptides as a data transfer medium.

The most unusual aspect of this spacecraft is its ability to change shape depending on its operational mode. When traveling at high speed, the fins typically spread out toward the aft of the ship, suggesting an aerodynamic design possibly optimized for traversing the low-density matter of fluidic space. When halted, the fins fold forward into the main body of the craft. When powering up to discharge its energy weapon, the fins move to the vessel's midship as the vessel shortens in length and the "trunk" of the bioship beings to expand and glow.

BACKGROUND

The Borg's discovery of fluidic space and intrusion into it led to the discovery of Species 8472—this is the Borg designation for this race and the only identifier Starfleet currently uses. Unfortunately, Species 8472's first contact with life-forms from our galaxy was an assimilation attempt by the Borg. Protecting themselves, Species 8472 fought back fiercely and nearly destroyed the Borg. An unprecedented alliance with the crew of the *U.S.S. Voyager* helped the Borg develop a defense against Species 8472, utilizing modified Borg nanoprobes to attack Species 8472 and their ships at the cellular level. The nanoprobes would seek out the cells of Species 8472 and denature them, killing individuals and destroying their bioships.

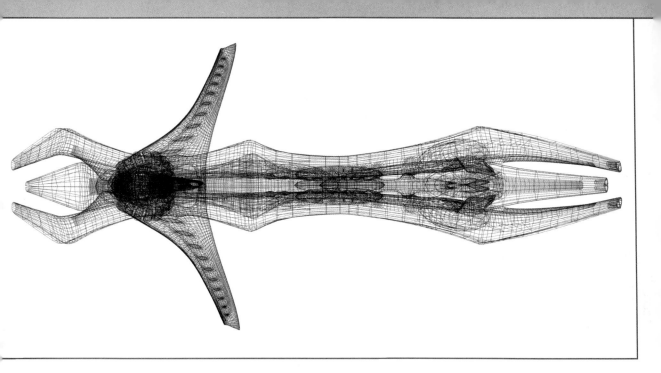

Fearing that the Borg and the Federation were planning an all-out offensive against them, Species 8472 attempted to infiltrate Starfleet. They began simulations in the Delta Quadrant to study the Federation more closely and prepare for a counteroffensive. Although this simulation seemed to make an escalation and ultimate confrontation inevitable, a peace offering by Captain Kathryn Janeway of the nanotechnology was able to defuse tensions. This demonstrated to Species 8472 that the Federation was not a threat. Starfleet has had no contact with Species 8472 since this encounter, but it is hoped that any future relations with this mysterious life-form will be friendly, thanks to the efforts of Captain Janeway and her crew.

SPECIFICATIONS

Dimensions:
  Overall Length: VARIABLE
  Overall Beam: VARIABLE
  Overall Draft: VARIABLE
Displacement: VARIABLE
Crew Complement: 1 "pilot"
Velocity:
  Cruising: UNKNOWN
  Maximum: UNKNOWN
  Acceleration: UNKNOWN

Duration:
  Standard Mission: UNKNOWN
  Recommended Yard Overhaul: UNKNOWN
Propulsion Systems:
  Warp: UNKNOWN
  Impulse: UNKNOWN
Weapons: UNKNOWN
Primary Computer System: UNKNOWN
Primary Navigation System: UNKNOWN
Deflector Systems: UNKNOWN
Embarked Craft (Typical): UNKNOWN

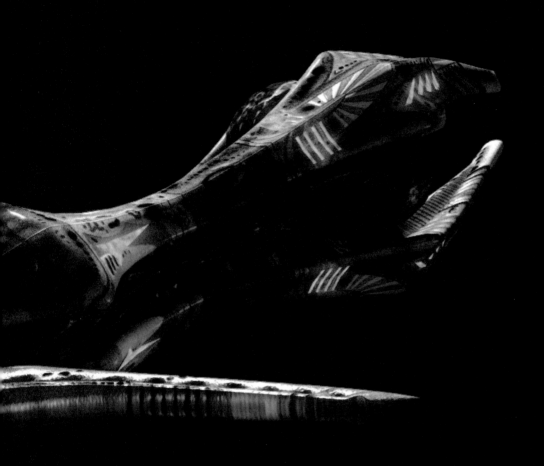

ARENA SHIP

DELTA QUADRANT ALIEN SPACE VESSEL   FIRST ENCOUNTERED: 2376

MISSION

Based in a sector of space inside the Delta Quadrant, the arena ship was a flying fortress dedicated to a single purpose: the combat spo[rt] of Tsunkatse. The arena ship traveled throughout the sector while beaming holographic coverage of an endless series of Tsunkatse matche[s] to billions of enthusiastic viewers on dozens of worlds. Unfortunately, not all of the Tsunkatse competitors were willing participants, and th[e] arena ship was known to kidnap unsuspecting space travelers and place them in the combat ring. For this reason, the arena ship was power[-] fully armed and heavily shielded. On the inside, a vast portion of the vessel was dedicated to holding cells and training facilities for contest[-] ants, while only a small area was devoted to the combat arena. An array of powerful transmitters studded the ship's surface and beamed [a] constant stream of Tsunkatse matches.

FEATURES

Closer in size to a small space station, the powerful arena ship was a significant adversary when encountered by the U.S.S. Voyager. Ove[r] five million metric tons, the arena ship dwarfed the starship. The immense size was backed by a series of advanced technologies designed t[o] make the ship nearly impenetrable. Reinforced hull plating was protected by tetryon-based covariant shielding. The uppermost deck of th[e] vessel, which housed the combat arena, was protected by an array of multiphasic force fields. The arena ship carried neutronic weaponry an[d] a specialized tetryon-based dampening field. This field, when used on smaller craft, could knock out power across multiple systems—com[-] munications, propulsion, weapons, shields, and transporters. Finally, the arena ship was an entertainment source for an entire sector of space[.] It had six signal generators beaming out a constant stream of holographic data to special arena complexes on numerous planets. The aren[a] ship allowed no spectators aboard, and the Tsunkatse competitors fought in a combat ring comprised of numerous holorecorders to captur[e] every move and angle.

BACKGROUND

Tsunkatse was a form of unarmed combat between two opponents, displaying their strength, speed, agility, and cunning. Each combatan[t] wore a pair of polaron disruptors on each of their hands and feet. These disruptors emitted a bioplasmic charge when they came in contac[t] with an opponent's targeting sensors. A competitor had to protect his or her own sensors while at the same time attempting to punch or kick those of the opponent. Extremely violent, Tsunkatse matches could also be deadly. While blue matches continued only until one competitor was knocked unconscious, red matches were stopped only when one combatant was dead.

On their way home through the Delta Quadrant, the crew of the U.S.S. Voyager was initially unaware both of the potential deadliness of this sport and also that many of the combatants had been captured and forced into the ring against their will. Powerful aliens from warrior races like the Hirogen, Pendari, and countless others had been kidnapped and made to fight. Voyager learned of this scheme when two of their own, Lieutenant Commander Tuvok and Seven of Nine, were captured and taken aboard the arena ship to fight. When Voyager con-tacted local planetary governments to inform them of this nefarious practice and seek their aid, most feigned concern while tacitly support-ing the practice and the revenue it generated. Unable to defeat the arena ship in battle, the combined weapons fire of Voyager and the Delta Flyer were able to knock out the arena ship's shields long enough to rescue Tuvok, Seven, and a Hirogen combatant.

The arena ship was damaged in the attack, and Starfleet assumed that repairs were made soon thereafter. When Starfleet vessels reach this sector of the Delta Quadrant, a general advisory will be issued.

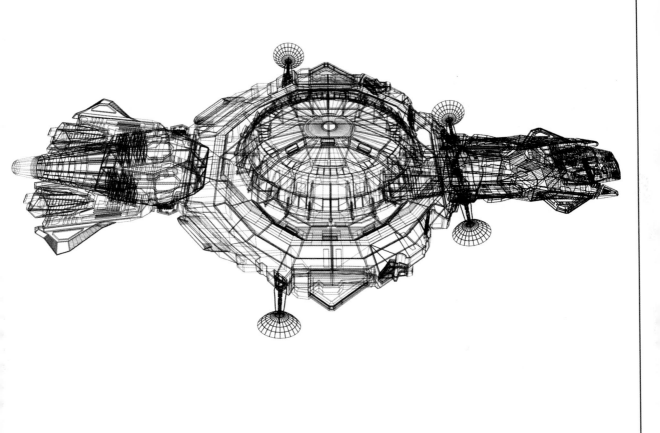

SPECIFICATIONS

Dimensions:
  Overall Length: 710.7 meters
  Overall Beam: UNKNOWN
  Overall Draft: UNKNOWN
Displacement: 575,000 metric tons
Crew Complement: UNKNOWN
Velocity:
  Cruising: UNKNOWN
  Maximum: UNKNOWN
  Acceleration: UNKNOWN
Duration:
  Standard Mission: UNKNOWN
  Recommended Yard Overhaul: UNKNOWN

Propulsion Systems:
  Warp: UNKNOWN
  Impulse: UNKNOWN
Weapons:
  Various Neutronic-Based Beam Emitters
    (TYPE UNKNOWN)
  General Energy Dampening Field Generators
    (TYPE UNKNOWN)
Primary Computer System: UNKNOWN
Primary Navigation System: UNKNOWN
Deflector Systems: Covariant Shielding and Multiphasic
  Force Field Generators (TYPE UNKNOWN)
Embarked Craft (Typical): UNKNOWN

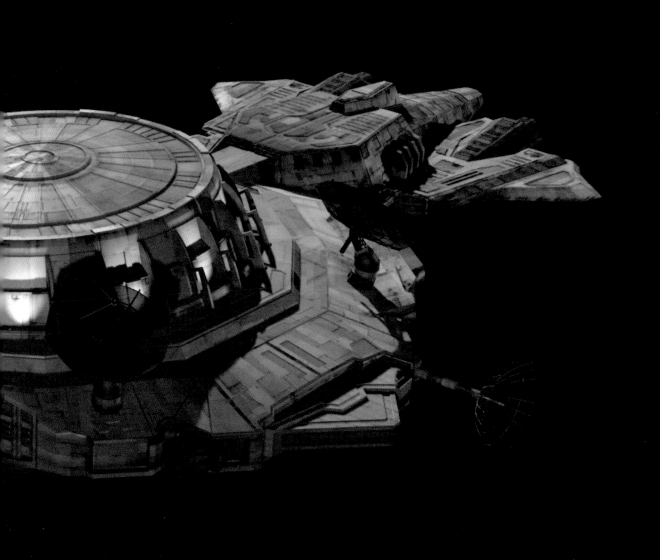

BORG QUEEN COMMAND SHIP

FIRST ENCOUNTERED: 2375

MISSION

Despite a number of encounters with the Borg little is known about this significant vessel. The majority of information that Starfleet has about the Borg is combined with extrapolation and conjecture. The Borg queen command ship appears to be a mobile command center for the queen to use as she coordinates the actions of the entire Borg collective. It is believed that the queen spends most of her time within the vast citylike Borg primary complex known as Unimatrix 01. Sometimes it is necessary for her to travel beyond the ship's confines. The command ship allows the queen mobility while still keeping her protected and in continuous contact with the collective.

FEATURES

Borg technology is constantly changing, adapting, and evolving as new races are assimilated into the collective. It is difficult to discuss the current state of any Borg technology, since any statement may be out of date by the time it is made.

Starfleet can make certain general conclusions about the Borg queen command ship. Smaller than a Borg cube by a volumetric factor of ten, the command ship can attain the critical warp velocity necessary to activate and enter a transwarp conduit. The command ship is heavily shielded, intended to protect the queen. The command ship is typically accompanied by an escort of Borg cubes. Modular components surround the central chamber that houses the Borg queen. Starfleet believes these modules, extending in a general diamond shape around the core, act as both communication relays and additional shield matrix generators. An enemy would have to cripple or destroy each of these heavily shielded nodes to gain access to the central chamber. The redundancy factors of these modules ensures that the queen will never be out of contact with the collective. The queen can apparently "die" and return. It seems reasonable to assume that the communication nodes can act to transfer her engramatic consciousness through the interplexing relay network of the collective and into a new Borg queen body.

The command ship appears to have the same capabilities as a Borg cube and sphere, including three modes of propulsion: sub-light, warp and transwarp. Transwarp coils allow the command ship to open thresholds in normal space to enter a series of transwarp conduits. It appears that a series of stable transwarp "hubs" are maintained throughout the galaxy. The command ship is highly maneuverable. Like most Borg vessels, the command ship is equipped with powerful photonic missiles that can be fired even within a transwarp conduit, high-energy particle emitters, and powerful tractor beams. Starfleet assumes the command ship to possess the highly effective cutting beam typical of a Borg vessel. Finally, the command ship supports a full complement of thousands of Borg drones, all serving the will of the Borg queen.

BACKGROUND

Starfleet first learned of the Borg queen when she approached Earth in an attempt to travel back in time and prevent Earth's first contact. At that time, she traveled in a cube. When it was destroyed, the Borg escaped into Earth's past in a sphere. The crew of the *U.S.S. Enterprise* (NCC-1701-E) managed to defeat the Borg. It is possible that this defeat inspired the Borg to design and construct the command ship as a faster, more heavily shielded vessel, with additional communications capability. The *U.S.S. Voyager* was able to destroy one such vessel, in the Delta Quadrant, in 2375 by collapsing a transwarp conduit while the command ship attempted to re-emerge into normal space.

Voyager's final encounter with the Borg in 2377 left the collective in shambles. But Starfleet makes no assumptions when it comes to the Borg.

SPECIFICATIONS

Dimensions:
  Overall Length: 820.4 meters
  Overall Beam: 820.4 meters
  Overall Draft: 820.4 meters
Displacement: 498,300 metric tons
Crew Complement: UNKNOWN
Velocity:
  Cruising: UNKNOWN
  Maximum: UNKNOWN
  Acceleration: UNKNOWN
Duration:
  Standard Mission: UNKNOWN
  Vehicle Maximum: UNKNOWN

Propulsion Systems:
  Transwarp: Multiple Transwarp Coil Assemblies
    (TYPE UNKNOWN)
  Warp: UNKNOWN
  Impulse: UNKNOWN
Weapons:
  Photonic Missiles (TYPE UNKNOWN)
  High-energy Particle Beam Emitters (TYPE UNKNOWN)
  Focused Cutting Beam (TYPE UNKNOWN)
Primary Computer System: UNKNOWN
Primary Navigation System: UNKNOWN
Deflector Systems: UNKNOWN
Embarked Craft (Typical): UNKNOWN

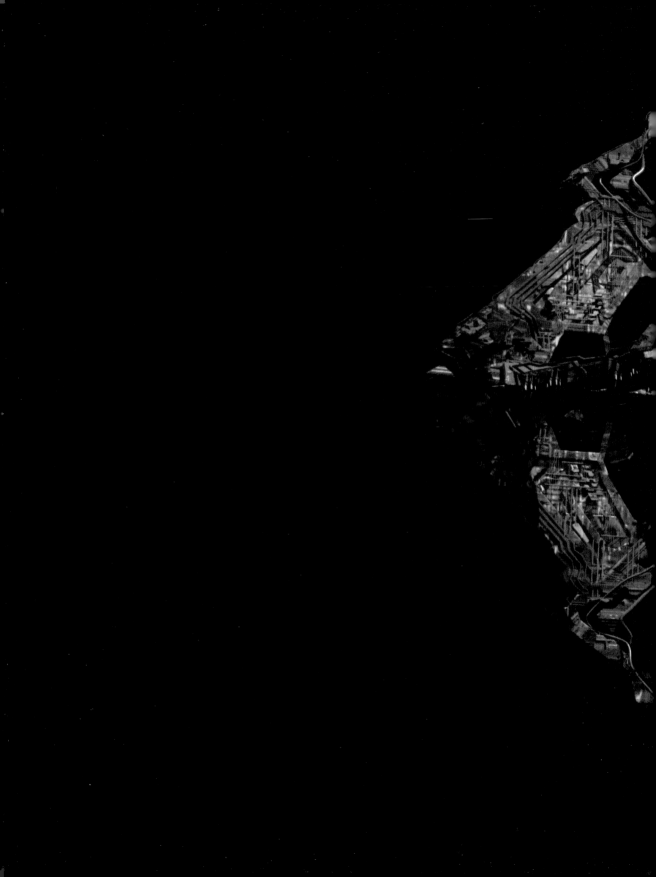

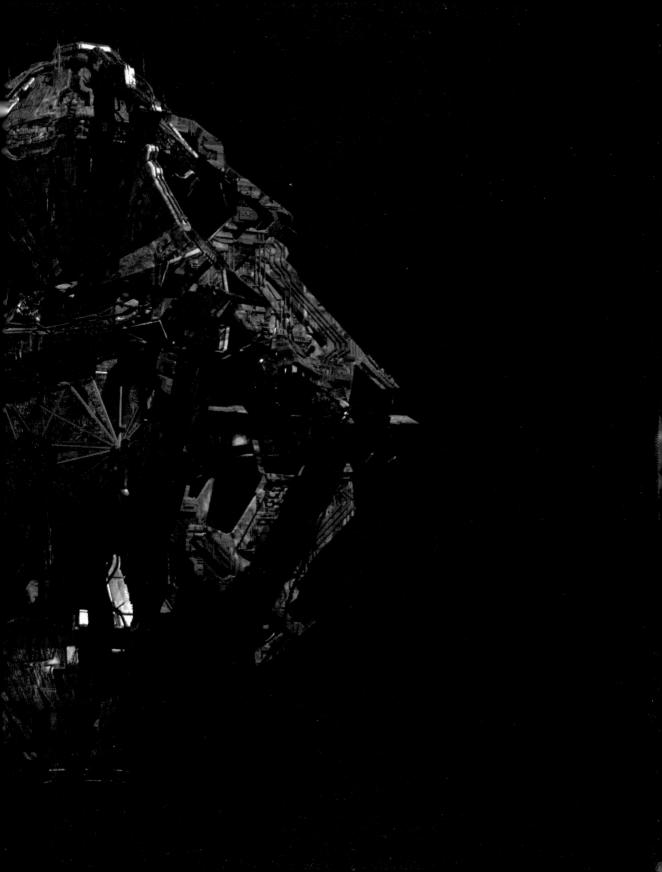

ACKNOWLEDGMENTS

Well, there are so many people that have helped with this book and inspired many other projects. Mojo, thank you for the opportunities. Without you, my position, the calendar and the books would be for naught. Doug Drexler, who has been an influence in my life (from afar and then close up!) since reading his *Star Trek* magazine when I was kid. It has been a pleasure working with him and I look forward to seven more years with him, helping to fly a starship. My Mom and Dad, who have supported and put up with my nonsense. Thank you to Ron Thornton, Mitch Suskin and Dan Curry, who have taught me so much. I would also like to thank Steve Pugh, John Gross, Karl Martin, Clark Acton, Gordon Forkert, Yosef Rosen, Mark Rosen, John Lima, Mike Okuda, John Eaves, Rick Sternbach, Pierre Martin Drolet, Koji Kuramura, John Teska, Janna Larson, Tracy Gromko, Sylvie Bordeaux, Ron B. Moore, Art Codron, Mark Bourcier, the writers of this book, Jonathan Lane & Alex Rosenzweig (thanks for the last minute work!), our wonderful editor Margaret Clark and, of course, Rick Berman, Brannon Braga, Peter Lauritson and the person who started it all, Gene Roddenberry. There are many others that cannot be listed in this space. Please know that you are all remembered and the influence has been felt.

Robert Bonchune
June 2001